對書中有疑惑的地方，

一定要查：

徹底了解，才容易背。

本書另有CD，
附在「一口氣背會話上、下集」中。
不斷地聽，誰都學得會。

你想和外國人交談嗎？

可至「台北市許昌街17號6F」（劉毅英文），

有「一對一」和「一對多」的課程。

英文老師在12分鐘內，

背完全書可得獎金*1*萬元，

可打電話預約口試。

電話：(02)2704-5525（學習出版公司）

5 秒鐘背 9 句，終生不忘記！

　　「一口氣英語」有十二冊，後來改編成「一口氣背會話」上下集，共 1,571 頁，現在隨手一翻，都讓我激動，如：You're doing great. (你表現很好。) great 是形容詞；You're doing a great job. (你做得很好。) doing 是及物動詞；You're doing well. (你做得很好。) well 是副詞。do 後面可接形容詞、名詞或副詞，學文法，光一個 do 都學不完，背了句子可以舉一反三，如你會說：You're doing great.，你就會說：You did good. 如果用傳統方式，誰敢說這句話？這個「精簡版」只有 208 頁，容易攜帶，可以隨身背。不懂的地方，可以查「一口氣背會話」上下集的「背景説明」。

　　背了又忘記，是人類學習語言最大的障礙。我們經過長時間研究，終於發現，只要將背好的東西再加把勁，變成直覺，就永遠不會忘記。「一口氣背會話」的發明，歷經千辛萬苦，根據編者的實際背誦經驗，一次一句、三句、六句，雖然容易背，但也很容易忘，一次九句最適合記憶，而且要特殊設計。像 2361-6101，這個電話號碼很難記，如果改成 2-361-6101，容易一點，但是，如果改成 211-311-411，這九個數字，就更容易記憶了。「一口氣背會話」就是根據這個原理研發而成。將每一回九句背至 5 秒內，就終生不會忘記。

　　美國人平常說的話，和他們所寫下來的文章，太多地方不同，由於書寫英文和口語英文不同，大部分美國人都不敢將他們平日所説的話，付諸文字，他們非常害怕寫錯，很害怕寫的東西不合文法，所以，大部分美國的出版品，不管是文章、小説、語言教材，與他們平時所説的話，格格不入。我們使用那些外國人編的語言教材，當然不容易說出來。

我看到一位學生家長，總是神采奕奕，我問她如何保養身體，她告訴我，她每天唸佛經，本來是看著佛經唸，後來唸得比看得快，最後不用看也可以唸，一天不唸就難過。「一口氣背會話」每個單元九句，練習到 5 秒鐘唸完，每一冊 12 個單元共 108 句，剛好 1 分鐘唸完。建議讀者把「一口氣背會話」每天大聲唸，一個單元練到 5 秒鐘之內，再唸下一個單元，到最後，不管早晚，對著牆上的時鐘，目標是 1 分鐘之內背完每一冊的 108 句。

　　我們每天不知浪費多少時間在胡思亂想，煩惱的事越想越煩，反而影響心情，也影響身體健康。「一口氣背會話」剛好解決了這個問題。編者自從每天自言自語背「一口氣背會話」以來，真是愉快。等人的時候背一背，不再無聊；跟別人意見不同的時候背一背，心平氣和。在台灣真好，每天自言自語說英文，路上碰到陌生人，都對你另眼相看，Speaking English well is a sign of success. 只要會說英文，就受到別人尊敬。

　　「一口氣背會話」的取材，經過再三研究，務必讓我們的讀者，背了之後，英語表達能力要勝過所有美國人，而且所背的英文也適合書寫。老師如果教學生，建議除了讓學生每個單元須在 5 秒鐘內背完之外，還可以要求他們默寫，這樣子同學又會說又會寫。英文會說、會寫以後，聽和讀還有什麼問題?!

　　　　　　　　　　　　　　　　　劉　毅

BOOK 1 每天要說的話

▶1-1 早上到學校見到老師、同學，都可說：

> Great to see you.
> So good to see you.
> What's going on?

▶1-2 上完課後，和老師說：

> Great class.
> Thank you, teacher.
> You are the best.

▶1-3 再稱讚老師說：

> You're an excellent teacher.
> Your material is great.
> Your methods are useful.

▶1-4 老師可以鼓勵同學，同學也可以鼓勵同學：

> You're doing fine.
> You got it.
> Keep on going.

▶1-5 下課後，邀請同學一起走：

> Let's go.
> Let's jet.
> Let's get out of here.

▶1-6 回家路上，可邀請同學吃東西：

> Let's grab a bite.
> What do you like?
> What do you feel like eating?

▶1-7 走到麥當勞點餐：

I'll have a Big Mac.
I'll have a small fries.
And a large Coke, please.

▶1-8 稱讚食物好吃：

Mmmmm. Mmmmm.
This is delicious.
This tastes great!

▶1-9 吃飽飯後說：

I'm full.
I'm stuffed.
I can't eat another bite.

▶1-10 提議散步：

Let's go for a walk.
Let's get some exercise.
A walk would do us good.

▶1-11 走累了說：

I'm beat.
I'm bushed.
I'm exhausted.

▶1-12 回到家說：

I'm home.
Home, sweet home!
There's no place like home.

1. Great to see you.

Great *to see you*.	很高興見到你。
So good *to see you*.	看見你真好。
What's going on?	有什麼事發生？
What's up today?	今天有什麼計劃？
What are you doing?	你要做什麼？
Anything exciting?	有沒有什麼好玩的事？
You look great.	你看起來很棒。
You look high-spirited.	你看起來精力充沛。
You look like you're ready for anything.	你看起來已經準備好做任何事。

** ——————————

go on 發生；繼續
exciting〔ɪk'saɪtɪŋ〕*adj.* 刺激的；好玩的
high-spirited〔'haɪ,spɪrɪtɪd〕*adj.* 精力充沛的
ready〔'rɛdɪ〕*adj.* 準備好的

2. *Great class*. (*I*)

Great class.	好棒的一課。
Thank you, teacher.	老師，謝謝你。
You are the best.	你最棒。
I like your class.	我喜歡上你的課。
I learn so much.	我學到好多東西。
You can really teach.	你眞是會教。
You're interesting.	你眞有趣。
You make it fun.	你上課很風趣。
You're a terrific teacher.	你教得很棒。

** ──────────

great 〔 gret 〕 *adj.* 很棒的
interesting 〔'ɪntrɪstɪŋ 〕 *adj.* 有趣的
fun 〔 fʌn 〕 *adj.* 有趣的
terrific 〔 tə'rɪfɪk 〕 *adj.* 很棒的

3. Great class. (*II*)

You're an excellent teacher.	你是個很棒的老師。
Your material is great.	你的教材真好。
Your methods are useful.	你的方法很有用。
You're never dull.	和你在一起絕不會無聊。
You're full of pep.	你充滿活力。
You keep us on our toes.	你讓我們專心上課。
I like your teaching.	我喜歡上你的課。
I like your style.	我喜歡你的方式。
You do a good job.	你教得真好。

** ——————————————

excellent〔'ɛkslənt〕*adj.* 優秀的
material〔mə'tɪrɪəl〕*n.* 資料；教材
method〔'mɛθəd〕*n.* 方法
dull〔dʌl〕*adj.* 乏味的；無聊的　　*be full of* 充滿
pep〔pɛp〕*n.* 活力　　*on one's toes* 警覺的
style〔staɪl〕*n.* 風格

4. You're doing fine.

You're doing fine.	你表現得很好。
You got it.	你知道該怎麼做。
Keep on going.	繼續努力。
That's the way.	你的做法對。
That's how to do it.	就是這麼做。
Don't change a thing.	不要改變。
Keep working hard.	繼續努力。
Keep doing great.	繼續好好地做。
Keep on doing what you are doing.	繼續做你現在正在做的事情。

**

do〔du〕v. 進展；表現；做
fine〔faɪn〕adj. 很好的　　　way〔we〕n. 方式；做法
keep on 持續；繼續　　great〔gret〕adj. 很好的；很棒的
change〔tʃendʒ〕v. 改變

5. Let's go.

Let's go.	我們走吧。
Let's jet.	我們走吧。
Let's get out of here.	我們離開這裡吧。
Where are you going?	你要去哪裡？
Are you heading home?	你要回家嗎？
Want to get a bite to eat?	要不要去吃點東西？
I'm hungry.	我餓了。
I could use a snack.	我有點想吃點心。
Let's go eat.	我們去吃吧。

**　*　———————————

jet〔dʒɛt〕*v.* 噴射　　***get out*** 離開

head〔hɛd〕*v.* 向～走去

bite〔baɪt〕*n.* 一口（食物）

use〔juz〕*v.* 使用；吸（煙）；喝（飲料）；吃（點心）

snack〔snæk〕*n.* 點心

6. *Let's grab a bite*.

Let's grab a bite.	我們去吃點東西吧。
What do you like?	你喜歡什麼？
What do you feel like eating?	你想要吃什麼？
You choose.	你選擇。
You decide.	你決定。
What do you recommend?	你推薦什麼？
How about McDonald's?	你覺得麥當勞怎麼樣？
It's fast and convenient.	它又快又方便。
What do you think?	你覺得如何？

** —————————————

grab〔græb〕*v.* 抓　　bite〔baɪt〕*n.* 一口（食物）
choose〔tʃuz〕*v.* 選擇
recommend〔͵rɛkə'mɛnd〕*v.* 推薦
McDonald's〔mək'dɑnḷdz〕*n.* 麥當勞（餐廳）
convenient〔kən'vinjənt〕*adj.* 方便的

BOOK 1

7. *I'll have a Big Mac.*

I'll have a Big Mac.	我要一個麥香堡。
I'll have a small fries.	我要一份小薯條。
And a large Coke, please.	還要一杯大杯可口可樂。
I'd like a milk shake.	我要一杯奶昔。
Make it strawberry.	要草莓口味的。
That'll be for here.	要在這裡吃。
Can I have extra ketchup?	我可以多要一些蕃茄醬嗎？
Can I have more napkins?	我可以多要一些紙巾嗎？
Thank you.	謝謝你。

** ─────────────────────

have〔hæv〕*v.* 有；吃   ***Big Mac*** 麥香堡
fries〔fraɪz〕*n. pl.* 薯條（= *French fries*）
milk shake 奶昔   strawberry〔'strɔ,bɛrɪ〕*n.* 草莓
for here 內用（↔ *to go* 外帶）
extra〔'ɛkstrə〕*adj.* 額外的
ketchup〔'kɛtʃəp〕*n.* 蕃茄醬
napkin〔'næpkɪn〕*n.* 餐巾紙（= *paper napkin*）

8. *This is delicious*.

Mmmmm. Mmmmm.	嗯！嗯！【注意語調】
This is delicious.	眞好吃。
This tastes great!	眞是可口！
I love it.	我太喜歡了。
The flavor is awesome.	味道眞棒。
It's out of this world.	太棒了。
It's mouth-watering.	眞是好吃。
I can't get enough.	我欲罷不能。
I could eat this all day.	太好吃了，我不會吃膩。

**

delicious〔dɪ'lɪʃəs〕*adj.* 好吃的
taste〔test〕*v.* 嚐起來
flavor〔'flevɚ〕*n.* 味道
awesome〔'ɔsəm〕*adj.* 很棒的
mouth-watering〔'mauθ'wɔtərɪŋ〕*adj.* 令人垂涎的

9. I'm full.

I'm full.	我吃飽了。
I'm stuffed.	我吃得很飽。
I can't eat another bite.	我一口也吃不下了。
I ate too much.	我吃太多了。
I need a rest.	我需要休息一下。
I need to take it easy.	我需要輕鬆一下。
I'll gain weight.	我會增加體重。
I'll get fat.	我會變胖。
I need to walk it off.	我需要散散步把它消耗掉。

** ——————————————

full〔fʊl〕*adj.* 吃飽的
stuffed〔stʌft〕*adj.* 吃得很飽的
bite〔baɪt〕*n.* 一口（食物）　　rest〔rɛst〕*n.* 休息
take it easy 放輕鬆　　gain〔gen〕*v.* 增加
weight〔wet〕*n.* 體重
gain weight 增加體重；變胖
fat〔fæt〕*adj.* 胖的　　*walk off* 以散步消除

10. Let's go for a walk.

Let's go for a walk.	我們去散步吧。
Let's get some exercise.	我們去做些運動。
A walk would do us good.	散步對我們有好處。
Walking is great.	散步很棒。
Walking is healthy.	散步有益健康。
It's the best exercise there is.	散步是最好的運動。
Where shall we go?	你說我們去哪裡？
Any place in mind?	你有沒有想到任何地方？
I'll follow you anywhere.	我願意跟你去任何地方。

** ─────────────

go for a walk 去散步
exercise〔ˈɛksə͵saɪz〕*n.* 運動
good〔gud〕*n.* 好處　　*do sb. good* 對某人有好處
great〔gret〕*adj.* 很棒的
healthy〔ˈhɛlθɪ〕*adj.* 健康的　　follow〔ˈfalo〕*v.* 跟隨

11. I need to go home.

I'm beat.	我好累。
I'm bushed.	我很累。
I'm exhausted.	我累死了。
I need to go home.	我必須回家。
I need to get back.	我必須回去。
I can't stay.	我不能留下來。
I have things to do.	我有事情要做。
I have to go.	我必須走了。
Let's call it a day.	我們今天到此為止。

** ——————————

beat〔bit〕*adj.* 疲倦的
bushed〔buʃt〕*adj.* 疲倦的
exhausted〔ɪgˊzɔstɪd〕*adj.* 筋疲力盡的
stay〔ste〕*v.* 停留
call it a day 今天到此為止

12. I'm home.

I'm *home*.	我回家了。
Home, sweet *home*!	家，甜蜜的家！
There's no place like *home*.	沒有一個地方比得上家。
I had a great day.	我今天過得很愉快。
Everything went right for me.	我每件事都很順利。
Today was really my day.	我今天運氣真好。
It's been a long day.	今天真是漫長的一天。
I did so much.	我做了很多事。
I learned a lot.	我學到了很多。

** —————————————————

sweet〔swit〕*adj.* 甜蜜的；舒服的
great〔gret〕*adj.* 很棒的　　　right〔raɪt〕*adv.* 順利地
go right 順利；進行順利

「一口氣背會話」經 BOOK 1

唸英文要像唸經一樣，每天大聲唸，從起床到睡覺，唸得比看得快，最後不看也會唸，養成習慣後，你會全身舒爽，你試試看，奇妙無比。

1. Great *to see you*.
   So good *to see you*.
   What's going on?

   What's up today?
   What are you doing?
   Anything exciting?

   You look great.
   You look high-spirited.
   You look like you're ready for anything.

2. Great class.
   Thank you, teacher.
   You are the best.

   I like your class.
   I learn so much.
   You can really teach.

   You're interesting.
   You make it fun.
   You're a terrific teacher.

3. You're an excellent teacher.
   Your material is great.
   Your methods are useful.

   You're never dull.
   You're full of pep.
   You keep us on our toes.

   I like your teaching.
   I like your style.
   You do a good job.

4. *You*'re doing fine.
   You got it.
   Keep on going.

   That's the way.
   That's how to do it.
   Don't change a thing.

   Keep working hard.
   Keep doing great.
   Keep on doing what you are doing.

5. *Let's* go.
   Let's jet.
   Let's get out of here.

   Where are you going?
   Are you heading home?
   Want to get a bite to eat?

   I'm hungry.
   I could use a snack.
   Let's go eat.

6. Let's grab a bite.
   What do you like?
   What do you feel like eating?

   You choose.
   You decide.
   What do you recommend?

   How about McDonald's?
   It's fast and convenient.
   What do you think?

7. *I'll have* a Big Mac.
I'll have a small fries.
And a large Coke, please.

I'd like a milk shake.
Make it strawberry.
That'll be for here.

Can I have extra ketchup?
Can I have more napkins?
Thank you.

8. Mmmmm. Mmmmm.
This is delicious.
This tastes great!

I love it.
The flavor is awesome.
It's out of this world.

It's mouth-watering.
I can't get enough.
I could eat this all day.

9. *I'm* full.
I'm stuffed.
I can't eat another bite.

I ate too much.
I need a rest.
I need to take it easy.

I'll gain weight.
I'll get fat.
I need to walk it off.

10. *Let's* go for a walk.
Let's get some exercise.
A walk would do us good.

Walking is great.
Walking is healthy.
It's the best exercise there is.

Where shall we go?
Any place in mind?
I'll follow you anywhere.

11. *I'm* beat.
I'm bushed.
I'm exhausted.

I need to go home.
I need to get back.
I can't stay.

I have things to do.
I have to go.
Let's call it a day.

12. I'm *home*.
Home, sweet *home!*
There's no place like *home*.

I had a great day.
Everything went right for me.
Today was really my day.

It's been a long day.
I did so much.
I learned a lot.

BOOK 2 買禮物去派對

▶2-1 邀請同學、朋友參加
　　　生日宴會時，可以說：

> I'm having a party.
> It's Friday night.
> I want you to come.

▶2-2 為了買生日禮物，要去購物中心買東西，需要問路：

> Excuse me, sir.
> I'm looking for a mall.
> Is there a mall around here?

▶2-3 到了購物中心買筆：

> I'm looking for a pen.
> I want a ballpoint pen.
> Do you have any good ones?

▶2-4 和店員討價還價：

> Can you lower the price?
> Can you make it cheaper?
> That's way too high.

▶2-5 買了筆以後，就去參加生日宴會：

> Happy birthday!
> Congratulations!
> You must be feeling great!

▶2-6 送禮物的時候說：

> Here's a little something.
> I got this for you.
> I hope you like it.

▶ 2-7 收到禮物時說：

Thank you so much.
It's wonderful.
It's what I always wanted.

▶ 2-8 收到禮物後，繼續再說感謝的話：

What can I say?
I'm speechless.
You shouldn't have.

▶ 2-9 稱讚別人送的禮物：

This is topnotch.
This is superb.
I'm very impressed.

▶ 2-10 收到禮物的人，可以繼續說：

I'm so lucky!
I'm really blessed!
I'm the luckiest person
    in the world.

▶ 2-11 宴會結束，問別人要不要搭便車：

Do you need a ride?
Can I give you a lift?
How are you getting home?

▶ 2-12 感謝別人開車載你：

Thanks for the ride.
You are a good driver.
I owe you one.

1. I'm having a party.

I'm having a party.	我要舉辦宴會。
It's Friday night.	時間是星期五晚上。
I want you to come.	我希望你能來。
You're invited.	我邀請你來。
Are you free?	你有空嗎？
Can you make it?	你能來嗎？
You gotta be there.	你一定要來。
You gotta show up.	你一定要出現。
It won't be the same without you.	沒有你就不一樣了。

** ———————————————

have a party 舉辦宴會
invite〔ɪn'vaɪt〕*v.* 邀請　　free〔fri〕*adj.* 有空的
make it 能來；成功；辦到
gotta〔'ɡɑtə〕【口語英語】必須（= *got to*）
show up 出現　　same〔sem〕*adj.* 相同的；一樣的

2. I'm looking for a mall.

Excuse me, sir.	先生，打擾一下。
I'm looking for a mall.	我正在找購物中心。
Is there a mall around here?	這附近有購物中心嗎？
I'm new here.	我對這裡不熟。
I don't have a clue.	我對這裡一無所知。
Can you tell me where it is?	你能告訴我在哪裡嗎？
Do you live here?	你住在這裡嗎？
Do you know this area?	你對這個地區熟嗎？
Any shopping center will do.	任何購物中心都可以。

** ——————————————————————

look for 尋找　　mall〔mɔl〕*n.* 購物中心
around〔əˈraʊnd〕*prep.* 在…附近
new〔nju〕*adj.* 不熟悉…的　　clue〔klu〕*n.* 線索
do not have a clue 一無所知　　area〔ˈɛrɪə〕*n.* 地區
shopping center 購物中心
do〔du〕*v.* 可以；行得通

3. *I'm looking for a pen*.

I'm looking for a pen.	我在找一支筆。
I want a ballpoint pen.	我要買一支原子筆。
Do you have any good ones?	你們有沒有什麼好的？
What's on sale?	有什麼特價品？
What's your best buy?	買什麼最划算？
Do you have any specials?	你們有沒有什麼特價品？
I like this!	我喜歡這個！
I'll take it!	我要買這個！
How much is it?	這個多少錢？

** ————————

look for 尋找

ballpoint pen〔'bɔl,pɔɪnt'pɛn〕*n.* 原子筆

on sale 特價   *the best buy* 最划算的貨品

special〔'spɛʃəl〕*n.* 特價品

like〔laɪk〕*v.* 喜歡；想要   take〔tek〕*v.* 拿；買

4. Can you lower the price?

Can you lower the price?	你能不能降低價格？
Can you make it cheaper?	你能不能便宜一點？
That's way too high.	那個價格眞的是太高了。
That's too expensive.	太貴了。
I can't afford it.	我買不起。
Please help me out.	請你幫幫我的忙。
How about a deal?	要不要給我一個好的價錢？
How about 20% off?	打個八折如何？
I'd really appreciate it.	我會非常感激。

** ────────────

lower〔'loɚ〕*v.* 降低　　price〔praɪs〕*n.* 價格
cheaper〔'tʃipɚ〕*adj.* 較便宜的
way〔we〕*adv.* 非常　　afford〔ə'fɔrd〕*v.* 負擔得起
help sb. out 幫助某人擺脫困難；幫助某人解決問題；
　　幫某人的忙
deal〔dil〕*n.* 交易　　***20% off*** 打八折
really〔'rɪəlɪ〕*adv.* 非常；十分
appreciate〔ə'priʃɪˌet〕*v.* 感激

5. *Happy birthday!*

Happy birthday!	生日快樂！
Congratulations!	恭喜！恭喜！
You must be feeling great!	你一定覺得很棒！
It's a big day.	今天是你的大日子。
It's your special day.	今天是你特別的日子。
We should celebrate.	我們應該慶祝一下。
Enjoy yourself.	希望你玩得愉快。
Have a super day.	祝你有美好的一天。
I wish you all the best.	祝你萬事如意。

**

congratulations〔kən͵grætʃə'leʃənz〕*n. pl.* 恭喜
great〔gret〕*adj.* 很棒的   big〔bɪg〕*adj.* 重要的
special〔'spɛʃəl〕*adj.* 特別的
celebrate〔'sɛlə͵bret〕*v.* 慶祝
enjoy oneself 玩得愉快   super〔'supɚ〕*adj.* 極佳的
wish〔wɪʃ〕*v.* 祝（某人⋯）   *all the best* 萬事如意

6. Here's a little something.

Here's a little something.	這是個小東西。
I got this for you.	這是我買來送給你的。
I hope you like it.	我希望你喜歡。
It's not much.	這不值多少錢。
You deserve more.	你應該得到更多。
You deserve the best.	你應該得到最好的。
You're one of a kind.	你非常特別。
You're so special.	你很特別。
You're really great.	你眞的很棒。

** ——————————————

little〔'lɪtḷ〕*adj.* 小的　　get〔gɛt〕*v.* 買；帶來
deserve〔dɪ'zɜv〕*v.* 應得　***one of a kind*** 特別的
special〔'spɛʃəl〕*adj.* 特別的
really〔'rɪəlɪ〕*adv.* 眞地　　great〔gret〕*adj.* 很棒的

7. *Receiving a Gift* (*I*)

Thank you so much.	非常感謝你。
It's wonderful.	這東西真棒。
It's what I always wanted.	這是我一直想要的。
It's perfect.	這個東西真完美。
How did you know?	你怎麼知道？
It's just what I needed.	這正是我需要的。
You're so thoughtful.	你真是體貼。
I'm really grateful.	我真的很感激。
I can't thank you enough.	我感激不盡。

** ─────────────────────

wonderful 〔'wʌndəfəl 〕 *adj.* 很棒的
perfect 〔'pɝfɪkt 〕 *adj.* 完美的
thoughtful 〔'θɔtfəl 〕 *adj.* 體貼的
grateful 〔'gretfəl 〕 *adj.* 感激的

8. *Receiving a Gift* (**II**)

What can I say?	我該說什麼呢？
I'm speechless.	我說不出話來了。
You shouldn't have.	你不該這麼做的。
I really don't deserve it.	我實在不敢當。
You're too good to me.	你對我太好了。
I really like this gift.	我真的很喜歡這個禮物。
It's very useful.	這個東西很實用。
I was going to buy one.	我本來要買一個。
You read my mind.	你真是了解我。

** ──────────────

speechless〔'spitʃlɪs〕*adj.* 說不出話的
deserve〔dɪ'zɝv〕*v.* 應得　　gift〔gɪft〕*n.* 禮物
useful〔'jusfəl〕*adj.* 實用的
read one's mind 了解某人的想法

9. This is topnotch.

This is topnotch.	這個東西眞高級。
This is superb.	這個東西太棒了。
I'm very impressed.	眞令我心動。
It's very nice.	這眞是好東西。
It's high quality.	品質非常好。
It must be worth a lot.	一定很值錢吧。
It's excellent.	這東西眞是好。
It's outstanding.	棒透了。
I like it so much.	我太喜歡了。

** ——————————————————

topnotch〔ˈtɑpˈnɑtʃ〕*adj.* 高級的；一流的（= *top-notch*）
superb〔suˈpɝb〕*adj.* 極佳的
impressed〔ɪmˈprɛst〕*adj.* 印象深刻的
quality〔ˈkwɑlətɪ〕*n.* 品質　　worth〔wɝθ〕*adj.* 值…
excellent〔ˈɛksḷənt〕*adj.* 優秀的；極好的
outstanding〔ˈaʊtˈstændɪŋ〕*adj.* 傑出的；很棒的
　　（= *very good*）

10. I'm so lucky!

I'm so lucky!	我真幸運！
I'm really blessed!	我真幸福！
I'm the luckiest person in the world.	我是全世界最幸運的人。
Everything is perfect.	一切都很完美。
Everything is going my way.	每件事都很順利。
You are the reason why!	就是因為你的緣故！
Thanks a bunch.	非常感謝。
I owe you a lot.	我非常感謝你。
I'm a lucky dog.	我真幸運。

** ——————————————

lucky〔'lʌkɪ〕 *adj.* 幸運的
blessed〔blɛst〕 *p.p.* 幸福的；幸運的
perfect〔'pɝfɪkt〕 *adj.* 完美的
go *one's* **way** 對某人有利　　reason〔'rizn̩〕 *n.* 理由
bunch〔bʌntʃ〕 *n.* 一堆；一把　　owe〔o〕 *v.* 欠

11. Do you need a ride?

Do you need a ride?	你要搭便車嗎？
Can I give you a lift?	我能送你嗎？
How are you getting home?	你要怎麼回家？
Let me take you.	讓我載你吧。
Let me drive you.	讓我開車載你。
It's no problem at all.	一點問題也沒有。
Ride with me.	和我一起坐車。
I enjoy your company.	我喜歡你陪我。
It'd be my pleasure.	這將是我的榮幸。

**

ride 〔 raɪd 〕 v., n. 搭乘；乘車   lift 〔 lɪft 〕 n. 搭便車
take 〔 tek 〕 v. 帶領   drive 〔 draɪv 〕 v. 開車載
not…at all 一點也不   enjoy 〔 ɪn'dʒɔɪ 〕 v. 喜歡
company 〔 'kʌmpənɪ 〕 n. 陪伴
pleasure 〔 'plɛʒɚ 〕 n. 快樂；榮幸

12. Thanks for the ride.

Thanks for the ride.	謝謝你開車載我。
You are a good driver.	你很會開車。
I owe you one.	我欠你一次人情。
I really appreciate it.	我真的很感激。
You've helped me a lot.	你幫我很多忙。
You've saved me a lot of trouble.	你幫我省掉很多麻煩。
Take care.	保重。
Drive safely.	開車要注意安全。
Catch you tomorrow.	明天見。

**————————

ride〔raɪd〕*n.* 搭乘　　owe〔o〕*v.* 欠
appreciate〔ə'priʃɪ‚et〕*v.* 感激
save〔sev〕*v.* 省去　　trouble〔'trʌbļ〕*n.* 麻煩
take care 保重　　safely〔'seflɪ〕*adv.* 安全地
catch〔kætʃ〕*v.* 抓住

「一口氣背會話」經 BOOK 2

唸「一口氣英語」要像唸經一樣，每天大聲唸，從起床到睡覺，唸得比看得快，最後不看也會唸，養成習慣後，你會全身舒爽，你試試看，奇妙無比。速度只要快到一分鐘之內唸完，就終生不會忘記。

1. I'm having a party.
   It's Friday night.
   I want you to come.

   You're invited.
   Are you free?
   Can you make it?

   You gotta be there.
   You gotta show up.
   It won't be the same without you.

2. Excuse me, sir.
   I'm looking for a mall.
   Is there a mall around here?

   I'm new here.
   I don't have a clue.
   Can you tell me where it is?

   Do you live here?
   Do you know this area?
   Any shopping center will do.

3. *I*'m looking for a pen.
   I want a ballpoint pen.
   Do you have any good ones?

   What's on sale?
   What's your best buy?
   Do you have any specials?

   I like this!
   I'll take it!
   How much is it?

4. *Can you* lower the price?
   Can you make it cheaper?
   That's way too high.

   That's too expensive.
   I can't afford it.
   Please help me out.

   How about a deal?
   How about 20% off?
   I'd really appreciate it.

5. Happy birthday!
   Congratulations!
   You must be feeling great!

   It's a big day.
   It's your special day.
   We should celebrate.

   Enjoy yourself.
   Have a super day.
   I wish you all the best.

6. Here's a little something.
   I got this for you.
   I hope you like it.

   It's not much.
   You deserve more.
   You deserve the best.

   You're one of a kind.
   You're so special.
   You're really great.

7. Thank you so much.
   It's wonderful.
   It's what I always wanted.

   It's perfect.
   How did you know?
   It's just what I needed.

   You're so thoughtful.
   I'm really grateful.
   I can't thank you enough.

8. What can I say?
   I'm speechless.
   You shouldn't have.

   I really don't deserve it.
   You're too good to me.
   I really like this gift.

   It's very useful.
   I was going to buy one.
   You read my mind.

9. *This is* topnotch.
   This is superb.
   I'm very impressed.

   It's very nice.
   It's high quality.
   It must be worth a lot.

   It's excellent.
   It's outstanding.
   I like it so much.

10. *I'm* so lucky!
    I'm really blessed!
    I'm the luckiest person in the world.

    Everything is perfect.
    Everything is going my way.
    You are the reason why!

    Thanks a bunch.
    I owe you a lot.
    I'm a lucky dog.

11. Do you need a ride?
    Can I give you a lift?
    How are you getting home?

    Let me take you.
    Let me drive you.
    It's no problem at all.

    Ride with me.
    I enjoy your company.
    It'd be my pleasure.

12. Thanks for the ride.
    You are a good driver.
    I owe you one.

    I really appreciate it.
    You've helped me a lot.
    You've saved me a lot of trouble.

    Take care.
    Drive safely.
    Catch you tomorrow.

　　　剛開始背「一口氣背會話」，也許困難一點。只要堅持下去，一
旦學會背快的技巧，就能一冊接一冊地背下去。每一冊108句中英文背
到兩分鐘之內，就變成直覺，終生不會忘記，唯有不忘記，才能不斷
地累積。

BOOK 3 搭計程車用餐

★

▶3-1 在大城市裡，招手叫計程車時，可以說：

Hey!
Taxi!
Over here!

▶3-2 剛到一個陌生的城市，可以問計程車司機，哪裡好玩：

I'm looking for fun.
Where is the action?
Where is a happening place?

▶3-3 想要再問計程車司機，哪裡有好的餐廳：

I need some help.
I'd like your advice.
Where's a good place to eat?

▶3-4 要下計程車時，可問司機車費多少：

What's the fare?
How much do I owe you?
How much should I pay?

▶3-5 到了目的地，你可以和同行的朋友說：

Here we are.
We are here.
We made it.

▶3-6 進到餐廳，看到接待員，就可說：

Table for two.
Nonsmoking section.
Can we sit by a window?

▶3-7 入座後，看完菜單，就可跟服務生說：

We're ready to order.
We know what we want.
Can you take our order now?

▶3-8 在餐桌上，可勸朋友多吃一點：

Eat up!
Eat some more!
Eat as much as you can.

▶3-9 當你喜歡一個地方的時候，就可說：

I like this place.
It's my kind of place.
It's just perfect for me.

▶3-10 在餐廳吃完飯後，要叫服務生來結帳，就可說：

We're ready.
We're done.
Check, please.

▶3-11 如果你想要去洗手間，可請你的朋友等一下：

Excuse me a moment.
I'll be right back.
Please wait for me.

▶3-12 約會結束，要和朋友說再見時，可說：

It's about that time.
It's time to say good-bye.
I have to get going.

1. *Calling a Taxi*

Hey!	嘿！
Taxi!	計程車！
Over here!	這裡！
How're you doing?	你好嗎？
Thanks for stopping.	謝謝你停下來。
Downtown, please.	請到市中心。
I just arrived.	我剛到。
I want to go downtown.	我要到市中心。
I want to see the sights.	我要看看值得看的東西。

** ─────────────────────

hey〔he〕*interj.* 嘿

downtown〔'daʊn'taʊn〕*n.* 市中心　*adv.* 到市中心

sights〔saɪts〕*n.pl.* 風景；名勝；值得看的東西

see the sights 觀光；看值得看的東西

BOOK 3

2. I'm looking for fun.

I'm looking for fun.	我在找好玩的地方。
Where is the action?	哪裡最好玩？
Where is a happening place?	哪裡最熱鬧？
I want some excitement.	我要找一些好玩的事。
Where should I go?	我該去哪裡？
Where do people go?	人們都去哪裡啊？
Please fill me in.	請告訴我詳情。
Please give me the lowdown.	請告訴我實際情況。
Can you introduce a good place?	你能不能介紹一個好地方？

**————————————

fun〔fʌn〕*n.* 樂趣；有趣的人或物
action〔'ækʃən〕*n.* 行動；活動
happening〔'hæpənɪŋ〕*adj.* 熱門的
excitement〔ɪk'saɪtmənt〕*n.* 興奮；刺激；令人興奮
　的事；好玩的事　　***fill sb. in*** 告訴某人詳情
lowdown〔'lo,daʊn〕*n.* 內幕；真相；實情
introduce〔,ɪntrə'djus〕*v.* 介紹

3. Where's a good place to eat?

I need some help.	我需要幫忙。
I'd like your advice.	請給我一些建議。
Where's a good place to eat?	想吃東西，去哪裡比較好？
I want good food.	我想吃好的東西。
I want a great meal.	我想好好吃一頓。
I want the best food around.	我想要吃附近最好的食物。
Where do the locals go?	本地人都去哪裡吃東西？
Where's a popular place?	大家喜歡去哪裡？
I want to eat where the locals eat.	我要去本地人吃東西的地方。

**

advice〔əd'vaɪs〕*n.* 勸告；建議
great〔gret〕*adj.* 很棒的   meal〔mil〕*n.* 一餐
around〔ə'raʊnd〕*adv.* 在附近   local〔'lokḷ〕*n.* 本地人
popular〔'pɑpjələ〕*adj.* 受歡迎的；討人喜歡的

BOOK 3

4. What's the fare?

What's the fare?	車費是多少錢？
How much do I owe you?	我該給你多少錢？
How much should I pay?	我該付多少錢？
Here you go.	拿去吧。
Here is one hundred.	這裡是一百元。
Just give me twenty back.	只要找我二十元就好。
Keep the rest.	其餘的你留著。
That's your tip.	算是你的小費。
Have a good one.	再見。

**───────────────

fare〔fɛr〕*n.* 車資　　owe〔o〕*v.* 欠

pay〔pe〕*v.* 付錢　　*Here you go.* 拿去吧。

rest〔rɛst〕*n.* 其餘的事物　　tip〔tɪp〕*n.* 小費

Have a good one. 再見。

5. Here we are.

Here we are.	我們到了。
We are here.	我們到了。
We made it.	我們到了。
This is it.	就是這裡。
This is the place.	就是這個地方。
It looks good.	看起來不錯。
Let's go in.	我們進去吧。
Let's check it out.	我們進去看看。
Let's give it a try.	我們試一試吧。

** —————————————————————————

make it 成功;辦到   *check sth. out* 調查;看看
give it a try 試一試

6. *Table for two.*

Table for two.	我們要兩個位子的桌子。
Nonsmoking section.	我們要非吸煙區的座位。
Can we sit by a window?	我們可不可以坐靠窗的位子?
Two menus, please.	請拿兩份菜單。
We're in a hurry.	我們趕時間。
We're pressed for time.	我們時間緊迫。
What's today's special?	今日特餐是什麼?
What's your best dish?	你們最好的菜是什麼?
What are you famous for?	你們以什麼菜出名?

** ————————————

nonsmoking〔nɑn'smokɪŋ〕*adj.* 禁煙的
section〔'sɛkʃən〕*n.* 區域
menu〔'mɛnju,'menju〕*n.* 菜單　　hurry〔'hɝɪ〕*n.* 匆忙
in a hurry 匆忙地　　press〔prɛs〕*v.* 壓
be pressed for time 時間緊迫
special〔'spɛʃəl〕*n.* 特餐　　dish〔dɪʃ〕*n.* 菜餚
famous〔'feməs〕*adj.* 有名的
be famous for 以～有名

7. *We're ready to order.*

We're ready to order.	我們要點菜了。
We know what we want.	我們決定好了。
Can you take our order now?	你現在可以幫我們點菜嗎？
I'll have the special.	我要點特餐。
She'll try the combo.	她要總匯。
We both want salads with that.	我們倆都要附沙拉。
Ice water for her.	她要冰開水。
Hot water for me.	我要熱開水。
That's it for now.	現在先點這些。

** ——————————————

ready〔'rɛdɪ〕*adj.* 準備好的   order〔'ɔrdɚ〕*v.,n.* 點菜
take one's order 接受某人點菜   have〔hæv〕*v.* 吃
special〔'spɛʃəl〕*n.* 特餐
combo〔'kɑmbo〕*n.* 綜合在一起的人或事物；總匯
salad〔'sæləd〕*n.* 沙拉   *ice water* 冰水
for now 目前；暫時

BOOK 3

8. *Eat up!*

Eat up!	吃啊！
Eat some more!	再多吃一點！
Eat as much as you can.	儘量吃。
Fill up!	儘量吃！
Keep eating.	多吃一點。
You can eat more than that.	你可以再多吃一點。
Don't be polite.	不要客氣。
You can't be full!	你不可能吃飽了！
You can do better than that!	你可以再多吃一點！

** ─────────────────────────

eat up 吃啊

as…as one can 儘可能（= *as…as possible*）

fill up 裝滿；變滿　　polite〔pəˋlaɪt〕*adj.* 客氣的

full〔fʊl〕*adj.* 充滿的；吃飽的

9. I like this place.

I like this place.	我喜歡這個地方。
It's my kind of place.	這是我喜歡的地方。
It's just perfect for me.	這裡非常適合我。
It's comfortable.	這裡很舒服。
I feel so relaxed.	我覺得非常輕鬆。
I feel right at home.	我覺得非常舒適。
What a nice place!	這地方真好！
I can be myself here.	我在這裡很自在。
I could stay here all day.	但願我能整天都待在這裡。

**

kind〔kaɪnd〕*n.* 種類   just〔dʒʌst〕*adv.* 很；非常

perfect〔'pɝfɪkt〕*adj.* 完美的；適合的

comfortable〔'kʌmfətəbḷ〕*adj.* 舒服的

relaxed〔rɪ'lækst〕*adj.* 輕鬆的

feel at home 舒適；感覺輕鬆

be *oneself* 舒適；自在   stay〔ste〕*v.* 停留

BOOK 3

10. *Check, please.*

We're ready.	我們準備要結帳了。
We're done.	我們吃完了。
Check, please.	請給我們帳單。
We're finished.	我們吃完了。
We're set to go.	我們要走了。
Please bring our bill.	請拿我們的帳單來。
We're all together.	我們一起結帳。
Do you take this card?	你們接不接受這張信用卡？
Do I pay you or the cashier?	我付給你，還是付給櫃台？

** ————

ready〔'rɛdɪ〕*adj.* 準備好的
done〔dʌn〕*adj.* 完成的；結束的
check〔tʃɛk〕*n.* 支票；帳單
finished〔'fɪnɪʃt〕*adj.* 完成的；結束的（= *done*）
set〔sɛt〕*adj.* 準備好的（= *ready*）
bill〔bɪl〕*n.* 帳單　　take〔tek〕*v.* 接受（= *accept*）
card〔kɑrd〕*n.* 卡；卡片　　pay〔pe〕*v.* 付錢
cashier〔kæ'ʃɪr〕*n.* 會計；櫃台；出納員

11. I need to wash up.

Excuse me a moment.	對不起，我離開一下。
I'll be right back.	我很快就回來。
Please wait for me.	請等我。
Nature's calling.	我內急。
I need to wash up.	我需要洗個手。
I need to use the facilities.	我需要上洗手間。
Where's the bathroom?	廁所在哪裡？
Which way should I go?	我該往哪裡走？
Where can I find a restroom?	哪裡有洗手間？

BOOK 3

** ────────────

excuse〔ɪk'skjuz〕*v.* 原諒
moment〔'momənt〕*n.* 片刻
nature〔'netʃɚ〕*n.* 自然；生理需求
wash up 洗手洗臉
facilities〔fə'sɪlətɪz〕*n. pl.* 衛生設備
bathroom〔'bæθ,rum〕*n.* 廁所
restroom〔'rɛst,rum〕*n.* 洗手間（= *rest room*）

12. *It's about that time*.

It's about that time.	時間差不多了。
It's time to say good-bye.	是該說再見的時候了。
I have to get going.	我必須走了。
I hate to leave.	我真不願意離開。
I don't want to go.	我不想走。
It's been a lot of fun.	和你在一起都很快樂。
You take care.	你保重。
You take it easy.	你好好保重。
Let's get together again real soon.	我們儘快再聚一下吧。

** ──────────────

get going 動身;離開
hate〔het〕v. 恨;真不願意;真不喜歡
fun〔fʌn〕n. 樂趣   *take care* 保重
take it easy 放輕鬆
real〔ˈriəl〕adv. 真正地;非常

「一口氣背會話」經 BOOK 3

　　唸「一口氣英語」要像唸經一樣，每天大聲唸，從起床到睡覺，唸得比看得快，最後不看也會唸，養成習慣後，你會全身舒爽，你試試看，奇妙無比。只背英文，速度快到一分鐘之內唸完，就終生不會忘記。

1. Hey!
   Taxi!
   Over here!

   How're you doing?
   Thanks for stopping.
   Downtown, please.

   I just arrived.
   I want to go downtown.
   I want to see the sights.

2. I'm looking for fun.
   Where is the action?
   Where is a happening place?

   I want some excitement.
   Where should I go?
   Where do people go?

   Please fill me in.
   Please give me the lowdown.
   Can you introduce a good place?

3. *I* need some help.
   *I'*d like your advice.
   Where's a good place to eat?

   I want good food.
   I want a great meal.
   I want the best food around.

   Where do the locals go?
   *Where'*s a popular place?
   I want to eat where the locals eat.

4. What's the fare?
   How much do I owe you?
   How much should I pay?

   Here you go.
   Here is one hundred.
   Just give me twenty back.

   Keep the rest.
   That's your tip.
   Have a good one.

5. Here we are.
   We are here.
   We made it.

   This is it.
   This is the place.
   It looks good.

   Let's go in.
   Let's check it out.
   Let's give it a try.

6. Table for two.
   Nonsmoking section.
   Can we sit by a window?

   Two menus, please.
   We're in a hurry.
   We're pressed for time.

   *What'*s today's special?
   *What'*s your best dish?
   What are you famous for?

7. *We*'re ready to order.
We know what we want.
Can you take our order now?

I'll have the special.
She'll try the combo.
We both want salads with that.

Ice water for her.
Hot water for me.
That's it for now.

8. *Eat* up!
Eat some more!
Eat as much as you can.

Fill up!
Keep eating.
You can eat more than that.

Don't be polite.
You can't be full!
You can do better than that!

9. I like this place.
It's my kind of place.
It's just perfect for me.

It's comfortable.
I feel so relaxed.
I feel right at home.

What a nice place!
I can be myself here.
I could stay here all day.

10. *We're* ready.
We're done.
Check, please.

We're finished.
We're set to go.
Please bring our bill.

We're all together.
Do you take this card?
Do I pay you or the cashier?

11. Excuse me a moment.
I'll be right back.
Please wait for me.

Nature's calling.
I need to wash up.
I need to use the facilities.

Where's the bathroom?
Which way should I go?
Where can I find a restroom?

12. *It's* about that time.
It's time to say good-bye.
I have to get going.

I hate to leave.
I don't want to go.
It's been a lot of fun.

You take care.
You take it easy.
Let's get together again real soon.

BOOK 4 搭機出國旅遊

★

▶4-1 打電話向旅行社訂購機票：

> I'm going to New York.
> I'm leaving next Friday.
> I'd like a round-trip ticket.

▶4-2 辦理登機手續時，要求坐好位子：

> I'm checking in.
> Here's my ticket and passport.
> I have two bags and one carry-on.

▶4-3 在飛機上，要求空姐服務：

> Could I have a blanket?
> Could I have an apple juice?
> Could I have a cup of hot water?

▶4-4 到達目的地出境時，與移民官說：

> Here's my passport.
> Here's my immigration form.
> My return ticket is inside.

▶4-5 在機場打電話預訂旅館：

> I'd like to book a room.
> I'd like to make a reservation.
> I need it for tonight.

▶4-6 到了飯店，辦理登記住宿：

> I have a reservation.
> I'm here to check in.
> What do I have to do?

▶ 4-7 打電話給房務部，要求服務：

Hello, housekeeping?
I'm going out for a while.
Could I have my room
cleaned right now?

▶ 4-8 搭巴士車去市中心，問司機路：

Does this bus go downtown?
How much does it cost?
How do I pay?

▶ 4-9 到站後，和司機或新認識的朋友告別：

Nice meeting you.
Nice talking to you.
I enjoyed our chat.

▶ 4-10 打電話，要求櫃檯晚點退房：

This is room 704.
I'm leaving today.
What time is checkout?

▶ 4-11 整理行李時，提醒同伴別忘記東西：

Are you all packed?
Are you ready to go?
Make sure you have everything.

▶ 4-12 打電話告訴櫃檯即將退房：

Hello, front desk?
I'm getting ready to check out.
I'll be down in ten minutes.

1. I'd like a round-trip ticket.

I'm going to New York.	我要去紐約。
I'm leaving next Friday.	我下星期五走。
I'd like a round-trip ticket.	我要一張來回票。
I want to go economy.	我要坐經濟艙去。
Do you have special fares?	你們有沒有特別的票價？
Do you have promotional rates?	你們有沒有促銷價？
My departure time is flexible.	我的出發時間很有彈性。
I don't mind a stopover.	我不介意中途停留。
I want an unbeatable price.	我要最棒的價錢。

**

round-trip〔ˈraʊndˈtrɪp〕*adj.* 來回的
economy〔ɪˈkɑnəmɪ〕*adv.* 坐經濟艙　　fare〔fɛr〕*n.* 票價
promotional〔prəˈmoʃənḷ〕*adj.* 促銷的
rate〔ret〕*n.* 價格　　departure〔dɪˈpɑrtʃɚ〕*n.* 離開；出發
flexible〔ˈflɛksəbḷ〕*adj.* 有彈性的　　mind〔maɪnd〕*v.* 介意
stopover〔ˈstɑpˌovɚ〕*n.* 中途停留
unbeatable〔ʌnˈbitəbḷ〕*adj.* 最好的；最棒的；無法擊敗的

2. Airport Check-in

I'm checking in.	我要辦登機手續。
Here's my ticket and passport.	這是我的機票和護照。
I have two bags and one carry-on.	我有兩件行李要託運，還有一件手提行李。
I want an aisle seat.	我要靠走道的座位。
I want to sit in the front.	我要坐前面的座位。
Can you get me a first row seat?	你能不能給我第一排的座位？
How about the emergency row?	緊急出口旁的那排座位怎麼樣？
Please try your best.	請你儘量試試。
I appreciate your effort.	辛苦了，謝謝你。

** ─────────────

check in 辦理登機手續　passport〔'pæs,port〕*n.* 護照
bag〔bæg〕*n.* 行李　carry-on〔'kærɪ,ɑn〕*n.* 手提行李
aisle〔aɪl〕*n.* 走道　front〔frʌnt〕*n.* 前面
row〔ro〕*n.* 排　emergency〔ɪ'mɝdʒənsɪ〕*adj.* 緊急的
try one's best 盡力 (= *do one's best*)
appreciate〔ə'priʃɪ,et〕*v.* 感激　effort〔'ɛfət〕*n.* 努力

3. In-flight Service

Could I have a blanket?	可不可以給我一條毯子？
Could I have an apple juice?	能不能給我一杯蘋果汁？
Could I have a cup of hot water?	能不能給我一杯熱開水？
I'm not in a hurry.	我不急。
It's not an emergency.	這不是緊急情況。
I can wait.	我可以等。
When do we eat?	我們什麼時候吃飯？
When do we arrive?	我們什麼時候到達？
How long till we get there?	我們還要多久才會到？

BOOK 4

** ————————————

blanket〔'blæŋkɪt〕*n.* 毯子　　juice〔dʒus〕*n.* 果汁
in a hurry 匆忙
emergency〔ɪ'mɝdʒənsɪ〕*n.* 緊急情況

4. Immigration

Here's my passport.	這是我的護照。
Here's my immigration form.	這是我的入境表。
My return ticket is inside.	我的回程機票在裡面。
I just arrived from Taiwan.	我剛從台灣到這裡。
I'm here on vacation.	我來這裡度假。
I have a tourist visa.	我有觀光簽證。
I'll be in the States for two weeks.	我將在美國待兩週。
I'll be staying at the Holiday Inn.	我將住在假日飯店。
Thank you for helping me.	感謝你幫忙。

**

passport〔'pæs,port〕*n.* 護照
immigration〔,ɪmə'greʃən〕*n.* 入境
form〔fɔrm〕*n.* 表格　　*return ticket* 回程票
inside〔'ɪn'saɪd〕*adv.* 在裡面　　*on vacation* 度假中
tourist〔'turɪst〕*adj.* 觀光的　　visa〔'vizə〕*n.* 簽證
the States 美國　　stay〔ste〕*v.* 暫住；住宿（旅館）
inn〔ɪn〕*n.* 旅館；飯店

BOOK 4

5. *I'd like to book a room.*

I'd like to book a room.	我要預訂一個房間。
I'd like to make a reservation.	我要預訂房間。
I need it for tonight.	我今天晚上要住。
I prefer twin beds.	我比較喜歡有兩張床的房間。
I'll settle for a double.	我可以勉強接受一張雙人床。
Do you have any vacancies?	你們有沒有空房間？
What are your rates?	你們的房間價格是多少？
What can you do for me?	你能幫個忙嗎？
Do you have a complimentary breakfast?	你們有免費的早餐嗎？

BOOK 4

** ————————————

book〔bʊk〕v. 預訂　　reservation〔ˌrɛzə'veʃən〕n. 預訂
make a reservation 預訂　　prefer〔prɪ'fɝ〕v. 比較喜歡
twin〔twɪn〕adj. 雙胞胎的；成對的
twin beds 兩張一樣的床；有兩張單人床的房間
settle〔'sɛtl̩〕v. 安頓；安定；安身　　*settle for* 勉強接受
double〔'dʌbl̩〕n. 雙人房；有一張雙人床的房間
vacancy〔'vekənsɪ〕n. 空房間　　rate〔ret〕n. 價格
complimentary〔ˌkɑmplə'mɛntərɪ〕adj. 免費的

6. *Hotel Check-in*

I have a reservation.	我已經有預訂了。
I'm here to check in.	我來辦理住房手續。
What do I have to do?	我必須做什麼？
How much is the deposit?	押金要多少錢？
Here's my credit card.	這是我的信用卡。
Should I fill out a form?	我該不該填寫表格？
I'd like a quiet room.	我想要一個安靜的房間。
I'd like a room with a view.	我要一個有景觀的房間。
Can I see the room first?	我可不可以先看房間？

BOOK 4

**

reservation〔͵rɛzəˈveʃən〕 *n.* 預訂
check in 登記住宿
deposit〔dɪˈpɑzɪt〕 *n.* 押金
credit〔ˈkrɛdɪt〕 *n.* 信用　　card〔kɑrd〕 *n.* 卡；卡片
credit card 信用卡　　***fill out*** 填寫
form〔fɔrm〕 *n.* 表格　　quiet〔ˈkwaɪət〕 *adj.* 安靜的
view〔vju〕 *n.* 風景　　first〔fɜst〕 *adv.* 先

7. *Hello, housekeeping?*

Hello, housekeeping?	喂，房務部嗎？
I'm going out for a while.	我要出去一會兒。
Could I have my room cleaned right now?	能不能馬上幫我打掃房間？
I'd like extra towels.	我要額外的毛巾。
I'd like a toothbrush and razor.	我要一支牙刷和一支刮鬍刀。
Please bring me a pot of hot water.	請拿一壺熱開水給我。
I have dirty laundry.	我有髒衣服要送洗。
I have clothes to be washed.	我有衣服要送洗。
What should I do?	我該怎麼做？

BOOK 4

** ————————————————

hello〔hə'lo, 'hʌlo〕*interj.* 喂
housekeeping〔'haʊs͵kipɪŋ〕*n.* 房務部
while〔hwaɪl〕*n.* 一會兒；一段時間
clean〔klin〕*v.* 打掃   ***right now*** 現在；立刻
extra〔'ɛkstrə〕*adj.* 額外的   towel〔'taʊəl〕*n.* 毛巾
toothbrush〔'tuθ͵brʌʃ〕*n.* 牙刷 razor〔'rezɚ〕*n.* 刮鬍刀
pot〔pɑt〕*n.* 壺   laundry〔'lɔndrɪ〕*n.* 待洗的衣物

8. Does this bus go downtown?

Does this bus go downtown?	這部巴士是不是去市中心？
How much does it cost?	需要花費多少錢？
How do I pay?	我該怎麼付錢？
I want the shopping district.	我要去購物區。
How long does it take?	需要多少時間？
How many stops are there?	要坐多少站才到？
Which stop is the best?	哪一站最好？
Please tell me where to get off.	請告訴我在哪裡下車。
Please tell me one stop ahead.	請在前一站告訴我。

BOOK 4

**————————————————

downtown〔'daʊn'taʊn〕 *adv.* 到市中心
cost〔kɔst〕 *v.* 花費　　pay〔pe〕 *v.* 付錢
shopping〔'ʃɑpɪŋ〕 *n.* 購物　 *adj.* 購物用的
district〔'dɪstrɪkt〕 *n.* 區；區域
take〔tek〕 *v.* 需要；花費（時間）
stop〔stɑp〕 *n.* （公車）車站　　 ***get off*** 下車
ahead〔ə'hɛd〕 *adv.* 在前面

9. *Nice meeting you.*

Nice meeting you.	很高興認識你。
Nice talking to you.	和你談話很愉快。
I enjoyed our chat.	和你聊天很開心。
Here's my number.	這是我的電話號碼。
Let's keep in touch.	讓我們保持聯絡。
Call me if you'd like.	如果你願意，打電話給我。
Good luck.	祝你好運。
Have a great one.	再見。
I hope we can meet again.	希望我們可以再見面。

BOOK 4

** ─────────────────────

meet〔mit〕*v.* 認識；見面
enjoy〔ɪn'dʒɔɪ〕*v.* 喜歡；享受
chat〔tʃæt〕*n.* 聊天
number〔'nʌmbɚ〕*n.* 號碼；電話號碼
keep in touch 保持聯絡　　***good luck*** 祝你好運
great〔gret〕*adj.* 很棒的

10. *Can I check out late?*

This is room 704.	這是 704 號房。
I'm leaving today.	我今天要離開。
What time is checkout?	退房時間是什麼時候？
Can I check out late?	我能不能晚一點退房？
Can I stay another two hours?	我可不可以多待兩個小時？
It would really help me out.	這真的會幫了我的忙。
That would be great.	那會很棒。
That would be a big help.	那會幫我很大的忙。
I'd really be grateful.	我會非常感激。

**

checkout〔'tʃɛk,aʊt〕*n.* 結帳退房
late〔let〕*adv.* 晚　　stay〔ste〕*v.* 停留
help sb. out 幫忙某人　　great〔gret〕*adj.* 很棒的
grateful〔'gretfəl〕*adj.* 感激的

11. *Are you all packed?*

Are you all packed?	你全都打包好了嗎？
Are you ready to go?	你好了沒有？
Make sure you have everything.	確定你東西都帶齊了。
Don't forget anything.	不要忘掉任何東西。
Don't leave anything behind.	不要忘記帶走任何東西。
Take a second look around.	再到處看看。
Check again.	再檢查。
Check one more time.	再檢查一次。
Better safe than sorry.	安全總比後悔好。

BOOK 4

** ─────────

pack 〔 pæk 〕 *v.* 打包　　ready 〔ˈrɛdɪ〕 *adj.* 準備好的
make sure 確定　　*leave ~ behind* 忘記帶走～
take a look 看一看　　around 〔 əˈraʊnd 〕 *adv.* 到處
one more time 再一次　　safe 〔 sef 〕 *adj.* 安全的
sorry 〔ˈsɔrɪ〕 *adj.* 遺憾的；後悔的

12. *I'm getting ready to check out.*

Hello, front desk?	喂，櫃台嗎？
I'm getting ready to check out.	我快要準備退房了。
I'll be down in ten minutes.	我再過十分鐘就下來。
Please send someone up.	請派個人上來。
Please check my room.	請檢查我的房間。
I haven't used the fridge.	我沒有用過冰箱。
I need to get to the airport.	我必須到機場去。
Do you have a shuttle bus?	你們有短程往返的公車嗎？
Do you have any suggestions?	你有沒有什麼建議？

** ────────────

hello〔hə'lo , 'hʌlo〕*interj.* 喂
front〔frʌnt〕*adj.* 前面的　　***front desk*** 櫃台
check out 結帳退房　　send〔sɛnd〕*v.* 派遣
fridge〔frɪdʒ〕*n.* 冰箱 (= *refrigerator*〔rɪ'frɪdʒə,retə〕)
get to 到達　　airport〔'ɛr,port〕*n.* 機場
shuttle〔'ʃʌtl̩〕*adj.* 短程往返的
shuttle bus 短程往返的公車
suggestion〔sə'dʒɛstʃən〕*n.* 建議

BOOK 4

唸英文要像唸經一樣，每天大聲唸，從起床到睡覺，唸得比看得快，最後不看也會唸，養成習慣後，你會全身舒爽，你試試看，奇妙無比。

1. *I'm* going to New York.
   I'm leaving next Friday.
   I'd like a round-trip ticket.

   I want to go economy.
   Do you have special fares?
   Do you have promotional rates?

   My departure time is flexible.
   I don't mind a stopover.
   I want an unbeatable price.

2. I'm checking in.
   Here's my ticket and passport.
   I have two bags and one carry-on.

   I want an aisle seat.
   I want to sit in the front.
   Can you get me a first row seat?

   How about the emergency row?
   Please try your best.
   I appreciate your effort.

3. *Could I have* a blanket?
   Could I have an apple juice?
   Could I have a cup of hot water?

   I'm not in a hurry.
   It's not an emergency.
   I can wait.

   When do we eat?
   When do we arrive?
   How long till we get there?

4. *Here's my* passport.
   Here's my immigration form.
   My return ticket is inside.

   I just arrived from Taiwan.
   I'm here on vacation.
   I have a tourist visa.

   I'll be in the States for two weeks.
   I'll be staying at the Holiday Inn.
   Thank you for helping me.

5. *I'd like to* book a room.
   I'd like to make a reservation.
   I need it for tonight.

   I prefer twin beds.
   I'll settle for a double.
   Do you have any vacancies?

   What are your rates?
   What can you do for me?
   Do you have a complimentary breakfast?

6. *I* have a reservation.
   I'm here to check in.
   What do I have to do?

   How much is the deposit?
   Here's my credit card.
   Should I fill out a form?

   I'd like a quiet room.
   I'd like a room with a view.
   Can I see the room first?

7. Hello, housekeeping.
   I'm going out for a while.
   Could I have my room cleaned right
      now?

   I'd like extra towels.
   I'd like a toothbrush and razor.
   Please bring me a pot of hot water.

   I have dirty laundry.
   I have clothes to be washed.
   What should I do?

8. Does this bus go downtown?
   How much does it cost?
   How do I pay?

   I want the shopping district.
   How long does it take?
   How many stops are there?

   Which stop is the best?
   Please tell me where to get off.
   Please tell me one stop ahead.

9. *Nice* meeting you.
   Nice talking to you.
   I enjoyed our chat.

   Here's my number.
   Let's keep in touch.
   Call me if you'd like.

   Good luck.
   Have a great one.
   I hope we can meet again.

10. This is room 704.
    I'm leaving today.
    What time is checkout?

    Can I check out late?
    Can I stay another two hours?
    It would really help me out.

    That would be great.
    That would be a big help.
    I'd really be grateful.

11. *Are you* all packed?
    Are you ready to go?
    Make sure you have everything.

    Don't forget anything.
    Don't leave anything behind.
    Take a second look around.

    Check again.
    Check one more time.
    Better safe than sorry.

12. Hello, front desk?
    I'm getting ready to check out.
    I'll be down in ten minutes.

    Please send someone up.
    Please check my room.
    I haven't used the fridge.

    I need to get to the airport.
    Do you have a shuttle bus?
    Do you have any suggestions?

BOOK 5 和老外看電影

▶5-1 介紹兩位朋友彼此認識：：

Do you know Andy?
Have you met Andy?
Let me introduce you.

▶5-2 向新認識的朋友介紹自己：

My name is Pat.
It's nice to meet you.
How do you do?

▶5-3 打電話約朋友出來玩：

When are you free?
What's a good time?
When do you want to get together?

▶5-4 向朋友建議去看電影：

I got a great idea.
Let's go out tonight.
Let's go see a movie.

▶5-5 和朋友討論看哪一部電影：

What's playing?
What's showing?
Anything really good?

▶5-6 到了電影院，排隊買票：

Pick a movie.
What looks good?
What are we going to see?

▶5-7 告訴朋友自己堅持要請客：

It's my treat.
It's on me.
Let me pay.

▶5-8 進了電影院裡面，和朋友挑選座位：

Where do you want to sit?
Sit wherever you want.
Sit anywhere you like.

▶5-9 請旁邊的人小聲一點：

Please be quiet.
Please keep it down.
Could you lower your voice?

▶5-10 向別人道歉：

I'm sorry.
I apologize.
It's my fault.

▶5-11 和朋友討論剛看過的電影：

How was the movie?
What did you think?
Did you like it?

▶5-12 對朋友表達感謝：

What a great night!
I had a wonderful time.
I enjoyed myself a lot.

1. Let me introduce you.

Do you know *Andy*?	你認不認識安迪？
Have you met *Andy*?	你有沒有見過安迪？
Let me introduce you.	讓我替你介紹。
Andy, this is Pat.	安迪，這是派特。
Pat, this is Andy.	派特，這是安迪。
I'm glad you two could meet.	我很高興你們兩個能夠認識。
Andy is an old friend.	安迪是我的老朋友。
He is a great guy.	他是個好人。
You two have a lot in common.	你們兩個有很多共同點。

BOOK 5

** ————————————

know〔no〕*v.* 知道；認識   Andy〔'ændɪ〕*n.* 安迪 (男子名)

meet〔mit〕*v.* 會面；認識

introduce〔͵ɪntrə'djus〕*v.* 介紹

Pat〔pæt〕*n.* 派特 (男子名或女子名皆可)

glad〔glæd〕*adj.* 高興的   great〔gret〕*adj.* 很棒的

guy〔gaɪ〕*n.* 人   *have a lot in common* 有很多共同點

2. How do you do?

My name is Pat.	我的名字是派特。
It's nice to meet you.	很高興認識你。
How do you do?	你好。
I'm from Taiwan.	我是台灣人。
I'm a student.	我是個學生。
How about you?	你呢？
Where are you from?	你是哪裡人？
What do you do?	你從事什麼行業？
Been here long?	你在這裡很久了嗎？

**────────────────

meet〔mit〕v. 認識

3. When are you free?

When are you free?	你什麼時候有空？
What's a good time?	什麼時候好呢？
When do you want to get together?	你要什麼時候碰面呢？
Anytime is OK.	任何時間都可以。
Just let me know.	只要告訴我就好了。
I'll be there for sure.	我一定會到。
Where shall we meet?	我們在哪裡見面好呢？
Where's a good place?	什麼地方好呢？
I don't want to miss you.	我不想遇不到你。

BOOK 5

** ——————————————

free〔fri〕*adj.* 有空的   *get together* 聚會
let sb. know 告訴某人   *for sure* 一定
miss〔mɪs〕*v.* 錯過；沒找到；沒遇到

4. *Let's go see a movie*.

I got a great idea.	我有一個很棒的點子。
Let's go out tonight.	我們今晚出去吧。
Let's go see a movie.	我們去看電影吧。
It's been a long time.	已經好久了。
We need to relax.	我們需要放鬆一下。
We need to do something new.	我們需要做一些新的事情。
What do you say?	你覺得怎麼樣？
How do you feel?	你覺得怎麼樣？
How does a movie sound?	看電影怎麼樣？

BOOK 5

** ────────────────

I got 我有　　great〔gret〕*adj.* 很棒的
idea〔aɪˈdiə〕*n.* 主意；點子
relax〔rɪˈlæks〕*v.* 放鬆　　sound〔saʊnd〕*v.* 聽起來

5. *What's playing?*

What's playing?	在上演什麼電影？
What's showing?	在上演什麼電影？
Anything really good?	有什麼真的好看的電影？
What choices do we have?	我們有什麼可以選？
What do you want to see?	你想看什麼電影？
What times are the shows?	電影什麼時候開演？
You choose the movie.	你來選擇電影。
I'll let you decide.	我讓你決定。
I'm game for anything.	我什麼都願意。

BOOK 5

** ─────────

play〔ple〕*v.*（戲、電影等）上演；上映

show〔ʃo〕*v.*（電影）上映；（戲劇）演出　*n.* 戲；電影

choice〔tʃɔɪs〕*n.* 選擇　　time〔taɪm〕*n.* 時刻

choose〔tʃuz〕*v.* 選擇　　decide〔dɪ'saɪd〕*v.* 決定

game〔gem〕*adj.* 願意的

6. *Pick a movie.*

Pick a movie.	挑一部電影。
What looks good?	哪部電影看起來好呢？
What are we going to see?	我們要看什麼電影？
I'll wait in line.	我去排隊。
I'll get the tickets.	我去買票。
Why don't you go take a look around?	你何不到處去看看？
See what's going on.	去隨便看看。
See what they have.	看看他們有什麼。
Check out the food court.	看看美食廣場有什麼好吃的。

** ——————————————

pick〔pɪk〕*v.* 挑選　　*wait in line* 排隊
get〔gɛt〕*v.* 買　　*take a look* 看一看
around〔ə'raʊnd〕*adv.* 四處
be going on 進行；發生　　*check out* 看看
court〔kort〕*n.* 庭院
food court （購物中心的）小吃街；美食廣場

7. *It's my treat.*

It's my treat.	我請客。
It's on me.	我請客。
Let me pay.	讓我付錢。
Be my guest.	我請客。
*I'*m paying.	我來付錢。
I got it.	我買單。
Don't say a word.	不要爭。
It's my pleasure.	這是我的榮幸。
Next time you can pay.	下次你可以付。

BOOK 5

** ————————————

treat〔trit〕*n.* 招待；請客
pay〔pe〕*v.* 付錢   guest〔gɛst〕*n.* 客人
Be my guest. 我請客。
word〔wɝd〕*n.* 話   pleasure〔'plɛʒɚ〕*n.* 榮幸
next time 下一次

8. *Where do you want to sit?*

Where do you want to sit?	你想坐在哪裡？
Sit wherever you want.	坐任何你想要坐的地方。
Sit anywhere you like.	坐任何你喜歡坐的地方。
I'm not picky.	我不挑剔。
You call the shots.	由你決定。
Any place is fine with me.	我任何地方都可以。
There's a nice spot.	有一個好地方。
No one will bother us.	沒有人會打擾我們。
We can stay away from the crowd.	我們可以避開人多的地方。

BOOK 5

** ————————————

picky〔ˈpɪkɪ〕*adj.* 挑剔的　　shot〔ʃɑt〕*n.* 發射
call the shots 發號施令；做決定
spot〔spɑt〕*n.* 地點；場所；地方
bother〔ˈbɑðɚ〕*v.* 打擾　　*stay away from* 遠離
crowd〔kraud〕*n.* 人群

9. *Please be quiet*.

Please be quiet.	請安靜一點。
Please keep it down.	說話請小聲一點。
Could you lower your voice?	你能不能把聲音降低一點？
You're too loud.	你太大聲了。
You're too noisy.	你太吵了。
You're disturbing everybody.	你打擾到大家了。
Sorry to say that.	很抱歉我那麼說。
I hope you don't mind.	我希望你不要介意。
Please don't take offense.	請不要生氣。

BOOK 5

** ——————————

quiet〔'kwaɪət〕*adj.* 安靜的　　lower〔'loɚ〕*v.* 降低
voice〔vɔɪs〕*n.* 聲音　　loud〔laʊd〕*adj.* 大聲的
noisy〔'nɔɪzɪ〕*adj.* 吵鬧的
disturb〔dɪ'stɝb〕*v.* 打擾　　mind〔maɪnd〕*v.* 介意
offense〔ə'fɛns〕*n.* 冒犯　　*take offense* 生氣

10. I'm sorry.

I'm sorry.	我很抱歉。
I apologize.	我道歉。
It's my fault.	是我的錯。
I was wrong.	我當時錯了。
You are right.	你是對的。
Please forgive me.	請原諒我。
I didn't mean it.	我不是有意的。
It wasn't on purpose.	那不是故意的。
It won't happen again.	這種事不會再發生了。

** ─────────────────────

apologize〔ə'pɑlə,dʒaɪz〕v. 道歉
fault〔fɔlt〕n. 過錯　　forgive〔fɚ'gɪv〕v. 原諒
mean〔min〕v. 有…的意思；本意是
purpose〔'pɝpəs〕n. 目的
on purpose 故意地　　happen〔'hæpən〕v. 發生

11. How was the movie?

How was the movie? 電影怎麼樣？

What did you think? 你認爲怎麼樣？

Did you like it? 你喜歡嗎？

I thought it was terrific. 我認爲很棒。

I really enjoyed it. 我眞的很喜歡。

I highly recommend it. 我非常推薦它。

It was worth it. 它是值得的。

It was very entertaining. 它非常有趣。

I give it two thumbs up. 我給它最高的評價。

BOOK 5

** ―――――――――――――――

terrific〔təˈrɪfɪk〕*adj.* 很棒的

enjoy〔ɪnˈdʒɔɪ〕*v.* 喜歡

highly〔ˈhaɪlɪ〕*adv.* 非常；高度（地）

recommend〔ˌrɛkəˈmɛnd〕*v.* 推薦

worth〔wɝθ〕*adj.* 值得的　　thumb〔θʌm〕*n.* 大拇指

12. *What a great night!*

What a great night!	多麼美好的一個晚上！
I had a wonderful time.	我玩得好愉快。
I enjoyed myself a lot.	我玩得很愉快。
You're good company.	和你在一起很快樂。
You're fun to be with.	和你在一起很愉快。
I like hanging out with you.	我喜歡和你在一起。
Thanks for tonight.	感謝你今天晚上的一切。
Let's do it again.	我們下次再約。
I'm lucky to have a friend like you.	我真幸運，有像你這樣的朋友。

BOOK 5

** ───────────────

great 〔 gret 〕 *adj.* 很棒的
wonderful 〔'wʌndəfəl 〕 *adj.* 很棒的
enjoy oneself 玩得愉快
company 〔'kʌmpənɪ 〕 *n.* 同伴　　fun 〔 fʌn 〕 *adj.* 有趣的
hang out with 和～在一起　　lucky 〔'lʌkɪ 〕 *adj.* 幸運的

「一口氣背會話」經 BOOK 5

唸英文要像唸經一樣，每天大聲唸，從起床到睡覺，唸得比看得快，最後不看也會唸，養成習慣後，你會全身舒爽，你試試看，奇妙無比。

1. Do you know *Andy*?
   Have you met *Andy*?
   Let me introduce you.

   Andy, this is Pat.
   Pat, this is Andy.
   I'm glad you two could meet.

   Andy is an old friend.
   He is a great guy.
   You two have a lot in common.

2. My name is Pat.
   It's nice to meet you.
   How do you do?

   I'm from Taiwan.
   I'm a student.
   How about you?

   Where are you from?
   What do you do?
   Been here long?

3. When are you free?
   What's a good time?
   When do you want to get together?

   Anytime is OK.
   Just let me know.
   I'll be there for sure.

   Where shall we meet?
   Where's a good place?
   I don't want to miss you.

4. I got a great idea.
   Let's go out tonight.
   Let's go see a movie.

   It's been a long time.
   We need to relax.
   We need to do something new.

   What do you say?
   How do you feel?
   How does a movie sound?

5. *What's* playing?
   What's showing?
   Anything really good?

   What choices do we have?
   What do you want to see?
   What times are the shows?

   You choose the movie.
   I'll let you decide.
   I'm game for anything.

6. Pick a movie.
   What looks good?
   What are we going to see?

   I'll wait in line.
   I'll get the tickets.
   Why don't you go take a look around?

   See what's going on.
   See what they have.
   Check out the food court.

7. *It's* my treat.
    It's on me.
    Let me pay.

    Be my guest.
    I'm paying.
    I got it.

    Don't say a word.
    It's my pleasure.
    Next time you can pay.

8. Where do you want to sit?
    Sit wherever you want.
    Sit anywhere you like.

    I'm not picky.
    You call the shots.
    Any place is fine with me.

    There's a nice spot.
    No one will bother us.
    We can stay away from the crowd.

9. *Please* be quiet.
    Please keep it down.
    Could you lower your voice?

    You're too loud.
    You're too noisy.
    You're disturbing everybody.

    Sorry to say that.
    I hope you don't mind.
    Please don't take offense.

10. *I'm* sorry.
    I apologize.
    It's my fault.

    I was wrong.
    You are right.
    Please forgive me.

    I didn't mean it.
    It wasn't on purpose.
    It won't happen again.

11. How was the movie?
    What did you think?
    Did you like it?

    I thought it was terrific.
    I really enjoyed it.
    I highly recommend it.

    It was worth it.
    It was very entertaining.
    I give it two thumbs up.

12. What a great night!
    I had a wonderful time.
    I enjoyed myself a lot.

    You're good company.
    You're fun to be with.
    I like hanging out with you.

    Thanks for tonight.
    Let's do it again.
    I'm lucky to have a friend like you.

BOOK 6 帶老外去郊遊

▶6-1 到了禮拜五的時候，就可以跟朋友說：

Thank God it's Friday.
The weekend is here.
We made it through the week.

▶6-2 另一位朋友，就可以回答說：

I agree.
I'm with you.
You're absolutely right.

▶6-3 你可以接著跟朋友說：

What can we do?
Where should we go?
Where's a great place?

▶6-4 你可以提議說：

Let's go hiking.
Let's head for the hills.
Let's leave the city behind.

▶6-5 你可以再跟朋友說：

Let's get ready.
Let's make a plan.
It's better to be prepared.

▶6-6 你可以邀請朋友上你的車：

Please get in.
Sit up front.
Feel free to adjust the seat.

▶6-7 在車子裡面，看到油表顯示汽油不夠，你就對朋友說：

We need gas.
We're on empty.
We're running out of gas.

▶6-8 在加油站和服務人員說：

Hi!
Twenty bucks, please.
Make it regular.

▶6-9 兩個人在爬山，你叫你的朋友趕快跟你走：

Hurry up!
Move faster.
Pick it up.

▶6-10 你可以鼓勵走不動的人說：

You can do it.
You have what it takes.
I believe in you.

▶6-11 在山上看到很好的風景，就說：

Wow!
What a view!
It's really awesome!

▶6-12 晚上你的朋友要下車了，你就跟他說：

Good night.
Sleep well.
Sweet dreams.

1. Thank God it's Friday.

Thank God it's Friday.	謝天謝地，今天是星期五。
The weekend is here.	週末到了。
We made it through the week.	我們熬過了這個禮拜。
I'm psyched.	我很興奮。
I'm very excited.	我非常興奮。
I'm all fired up.	我非常興奮。
Let's get away.	我們去玩吧。
Let's do something special.	我們做一些特別的事吧。
You only live once.	人只能活一次。

**————

God〔gɑd〕*n.* 上帝　　weekend〔ˈwikˌɛnd〕*n.* 週末
make it 成功；辦到　　*through the week* 整個禮拜
psyched〔saɪkt〕*adj.* 興奮的；已做好心理準備的
excited〔ɪkˈsaɪtɪd〕*adj.* 興奮的
fired up 興奮的；熱心的　　*get away* 逃脫；去旅行

BOOK 6

2. *I agree*.

I agree.	我同意。
I'm with you.	我支持你。
You're absolutely right.	你說得完全對。
That's for sure.	那是確定的。
That's the truth.	那是事實。
That's how I feel.	我也有同樣的感覺。
I feel the same way.	我有同感。
I couldn't agree more.	我完全同意。
You're right on the money.	你說得非常正確。

** ——————————————

be with 同意;和…一致;支持

absolutely〔'æbsə,lutlı〕*adv.* 完全地;絕對地

for sure 毫無疑問的;確定的

truth〔truθ〕*n.* 事實;真理

can't agree more 非常同意;完全同意

on the money 恰到好處;非常正確

3. *What can we do?*

What can we do?	我們能做什麼？
Where should we go?	我們該去哪裡？
Where's a great place?	哪個地方好？
Any ideas?	有沒有什麼點子？
Any suggestions?	有什麼建議嗎？
Anywhere is fine with me.	我去什麼地方都可以。
Let's go to the ocean.	我們去海邊。
Let's hit the beach.	我們去海灘吧。
I haven't been there in ages.	我很久沒去那裡了。

**

great〔 gret 〕*adj.* 很棒的

idea〔 aɪˈdiə 〕*n.* 主意；想法；點子

suggestion〔 səˈdʒɛstʃən 〕*n.* 建議

ocean〔ˈoʃən 〕*n.* 海洋

hit〔 hɪt 〕*v.* 打擊；到達；達到　　*in ages* 很久

BOOK 6

4. Let's go hiking.

Let's go hiking.	我們去郊遊吧。
Let's head for the hills.	我們去爬山吧。
Let's leave the city behind.	讓我們遠離城市的喧囂。
I can't wait to go.	我迫不及待要去。
I can smell the fresh air already.	我已經可以聞到新鮮的空氣。
There's nothing like Mother Nature.	沒有什麼能比得上大自然。
Rain or shine, we're going.	不管天氣如何，我們都要去。
Nothing can stop us.	沒有什麼可以阻止我們。
Maybe we won't come back.	也許我們不會回來了。

**────────────────────────

hike〔haɪk〕v. 健行；郊遊　　***head for*** 朝…前進
hill〔hɪl〕n. 山丘　　***leave ~ behind*** 遺留～；留下～
smell〔smɛl〕v. 聞到　　fresh〔frɛʃ〕adj. 新鮮的
air〔ɛr〕n. 空氣　　***nothing like*** 沒有什麼能比得上
Mother Nature（孕育萬物的）大自然
rain or shine 無論晴雨；無論情況如何
stop〔stɑp〕v. 阻止　　maybe〔'mebɪ〕adv. 也許

5. Let's get ready.

Let's get ready.	我們要做好準備。
Let's make a plan.	我們做個計劃吧。
It's better to be prepared.	最好要預先準備好。
We need supplies.	我們需要一些東西。
We need some stuff.	我們需要買一些東西。
Let's go grocery shopping.	我們去買東西吧。
Just keep it simple.	只要簡單就好。
Just stick to the basics.	要一切從簡。
Don't buy anything fancy.	不要買華而不實的東西。

** ──────────────

ready〔'rɛdɪ〕*adj.* 準備好的　　prepare〔prɪ'pɛr〕*v.* 準備
supplies〔sə'plaɪz〕*n. pl.* 用品；必需品；補給品
stuff〔stʌf〕*n.* 東西　　grocery〔'grosərɪ〕*n.* 雜貨
simple〔'sɪmpl̩〕*adj.* 簡單的　　***stick to*** 堅持
basics〔'besɪks〕*n. pl.* 基本原理；基本原則
fancy〔'fænsɪ〕*adj.* 精美的；昂貴的

6. *Please get in*.

Please get in.	請上車。
Sit up front.	坐到前面來。
Feel free to adjust the seat.	你可以調整座位。
Buckle up.	把安全帶扣上。
Fasten your seat belt.	扣好你的安全帶。
We don't want a ticket!	我們不想要罰單！
You can relax.	你可以放心。
I'm a safe driver.	我開車很安全。
I'll get you there in one piece.	我會平安地載你到那裡。

**　**

get in 進入；上車　　up〔ʌp〕*adv.* 向
front〔frʌnt〕*adv.* 向前面　*up front* 向前面；在前面
feel free to V. 自由地～　　adjust〔ə'dʒʌst〕*v.* 調整
buckle〔'bʌkl̩〕*v.* 扣上　*buckle up* 扣上安全帶
fasten〔'fæsn̩〕*v.* 繫上；扣上　*seat belt* 安全帶
ticket〔'tɪkɪt〕*n.* 罰單　relax〔rɪ'læks〕*v.* 放鬆
get〔gɛt〕*v.* 使到達　*in one piece* （人）平安無事地

7. *We need gas*.

We need gas.	我們需要加油。
We're on empty.	我們快沒油了。
We're running out of gas.	我們的汽油快用完了。
It's time to fill up.	該是加滿油的時候了。
It's now or never.	現在不加油就完了。
We can't get stuck here.	我們不能被困在這裡。
There's a station up ahead.	前方有個加油站。
They have both full and self-service.	他們有全面服務，也有自助。
Do you want to pump the gas?	你要不要加油？

** ————————————————

gas〔gæs〕*n.* 汽油（= *gasoline*〔'gæsḷ,in ,͵gæsḷ'in〕）
empty〔'ɛmptɪ〕*adj.* 空的　*n.* 空箱；空瓶；空桶
run out of 用完　　*fill up* 裝滿；在汽車油箱內裝滿油
stick〔stɪk〕*v.* 困住；使動彈不得；使進退兩難
station〔'steʃən〕*n.* 站【在此指 gas station（加油站）】
full service 全面服務　　self-service *n.* 自助
pump〔pʌmp〕*v.* 抽（水）　　*pump the gas* 加油

8. Gas Station

Hi!	嗨！
Twenty bucks, please.	請加二十元的油。
Make it regular.	加普通汽油。
Check the tires.	檢查輪胎，看有沒有氣。
Check the engine.	檢查引擎。
I think I'm low on oil.	我覺得我的機油不夠。
How does it look?	看起來怎樣？
What's the total?	總共多少錢？
Thanks for your great service.	謝謝你良好的服務。

BOOK 6

**

hi〔haɪ〕*interj.* 嗨　　buck〔bʌk〕*n.* 美元
regular〔'rɛgjələ〕*adj.* 普通的　*n.* 普通汽油
check〔tʃɛk〕*v.* 檢查　　tire〔taɪr〕*n.* 輪胎
engine〔'ɛndʒən〕*n.* 引擎　　total〔'totḷ〕*n.* 總額
great〔gret〕*adj.* 很棒的
service〔'sɝvɪs〕*n.* 服務

9. Hurry up!

Hurry up!	趕快！
Move faster.	走快一點。
Pick it up.	快一點。
Keep up.	要跟上。
Don't slow down.	不要慢下來。
Don't fall behind.	不要落後。
Keep pace with me.	跟著我的腳步一起走。
We can walk and talk.	我們可以一面走路，一面聊天。
I enjoy walking with you.	我喜歡和你一起走路。

**

hurry〔'hɝɪ〕*v.* 趕快　　*hurry up* 趕快
move〔muv〕*v.* 移動；走動　　*pick it up* 趕快
keep up 跟上　　*slow down* 減慢速度；慢下來
fall behind 落後　　pace〔pes〕*n.* 步調；速度
keep pace with 和…齊步前進；和…並駕齊驅
enjoy〔ɪn'dʒɔɪ〕*v.* 喜歡

BOOK 6

10. *You can do it*.

You can do it.	你可以做到。
You have what it takes.	你有能力。
I believe in you.	我相信你。
Hang tough.	堅持下去。
Hang in there.	要堅持下去。
Just keep trying.	只要繼續努力。
Go all the way.	要走完全程。
Go for the gold.	爭取第一。
Go as far as you can.	儘量發揮你的潛力。

** ─────────────

take〔tek〕v. 需要　　hang〔hæŋ〕v. 懸掛
tough〔tʌf〕adj. 堅硬的；不屈不撓的
hang tough 堅持下去；不洩氣
just〔dʒʌst〕adv. 只要　　try〔traɪ〕v. 嘗試；努力
all the way 自始至終；一直
gold〔gold〕n. 黃金　　*go far* 走遠；成功

11. Wow! What a view!

Wow!	哇啊！
What a view!	這景色真棒！
It's really awesome!	真棒！
I'm inspired.	我受到了鼓舞。
I'm glad I'm here.	我很高興能來到這裡。
*I'*ll remember this forever.	我會永遠記得。
What an amazing sight!	多麼令人嘆爲觀止的景觀！
What a special moment!	多麼特別的時刻！
It's like a dream come true.	它就像是夢想成真。

**

wow〔waʊ〕*interj.* 哇啊　　view〔vju〕*n.* 景色

awesome〔'ɔsəm〕*adj.* 可怕的；令人敬畏的；很棒的

inspire〔ɪn'spaɪr〕*v.* 激勵；鼓舞；使感動；給予靈感

glad〔glæd〕*adj.* 高興的　　forever〔fɚ'ɛvɚ〕*adv.* 永遠

amazing〔ə'mezɪŋ〕*adj.* 驚人的　　sight〔saɪt〕*n.* 景觀

moment〔'momənt〕*n.* 片刻；時刻

a dream come true 夢想成真

12. Good night.

Good night.	晚安。
*S*leep well.	好好睡。
*S*weet dreams.	祝你有甜美的夢。
Get some rest.	好好休息休息。
Have a good sleep.	睡個好覺。
Have a peaceful night.	希望你晚上睡得好。
See you in the morning.	明天早上見。
See you bright and early.	明天一大早見。
Tomorrow is a big day.	明天很重要。

**————————————

sweet〔swit〕*adj.* 甜蜜的；甜美的
dream〔drim〕*n.* 夢
rest〔rɛst〕*n.* 休息；睡眠　　sleep〔slip〕*n.* 睡；睡眠
peaceful〔'pisfəl〕*adj.* 寧靜的；平靜的
bright〔braɪt〕*adj.* 明亮的；發亮的；陽光燦爛的
bright and early 一大早（= *very early*）
big〔bɪg〕*adj.* 大的；重要的

「一口氣背會話」經 BOOK 6

唸英文要像唸經一樣，每天大聲唸，從起床到睡覺，唸得比看得快，最後不看也會唸，養成習慣後，你會全身舒爽，你試試看，奇妙無比。

1. Thank God it's Friday.
   The weekend is here.
   We made it through the week.

   I'm psyched.
   I'm very excited.
   I'm all fired up.

   Let's get away.
   Let's do something special.
   You only live once.

2. *I* agree.
   I'm with you.
   You're absolutely right.

   That's for sure.
   That's the truth.
   That's how I feel.

   I feel the same way.
   I couldn't agree more.
   You're right on the money.

3. What can we do?
   Where should we go?
   Where's a great place?

   Any ideas?
   Any suggestions?
   Anywhere is fine with me.

   Let's go to the ocean.
   Let's hit the beach.
   I haven't been there in ages.

4. *Let's* go hiking.
   Let's head for the hills.
   Let's leave the city behind.

   I can't wait to go.
   I can smell the fresh air already.
   There's nothing like Mother Nature.

   Rain or shine, we're going.
   Nothing can stop us.
   Maybe we won't come back.

5. *Let's* get ready.
   Let's make a plan.
   It's better to be prepared.

   We need supplies.
   We need some stuff.
   Let's go grocery shopping.

   Just keep it simple.
   Just stick to the basics.
   Don't buy anything fancy.

6. Please get in.
   Sit up front.
   Feel free to adjust the seat.

   Buckle up.
   Fasten your seat belt.
   We don't want a ticket!

   You can relax.
   I'm a safe driver.
   I'll get you there in one piece.

7. We need gas.
We're on empty.
We're running out of gas.

It's time to fill up.
It's now or never.
We can't get stuck here.

There's a station up ahead.
They have both full and
   self-service.
Do you want to pump the gas?

8. Hi!
Twenty bucks, please.
Make it regular.

Check the tires.
Check the engine.
I think I'm low on oil.

How does it look?
What's the total?
Thanks for your great service.

9. Hurry up!
Move faster.
Pick it up.

Keep up.
Don't slow down.
Don't fall behind.

Keep pace with me.
We can walk and talk.
I enjoy walking with you.

10. *You* can do it.
You have what it takes.
I believe in you.

Hang tough.
Hang in there.
Just keep trying.

Go all the way.
Go for the gold.
Go as far as you can.

11. Wow!
What a view!
It's really awesome!

I'm inspired.
I'm glad I'm here.
I'll remember this forever.

What an amazing sight!
What a special moment!
It's like a dream come true.

12. Good night.
*S*leep well.
*S*weet dreams.

Get some rest.
Have a good sleep.
Have a peaceful night.

See you in the morning.
See you bright and early.
Tomorrow is a big day.

BOOK 7 帶外國人逛街

▶ 7-1　下班後，你和你的朋友說：

> Let's hit the road.
> Let's get moving.
> Let's hustle out of here.

▶ 7-2　走到ATM(自動提款機)前，你可以跟你朋友說：

> Oops!
> Hold it a second.
> I almost forgot.
>
> I need to hit an ATM.

▶ 7-3　你從提款機回來，跟你的朋友說：

> Thanks for waiting.
> Sorry about that.
> Sorry I took so long.

▶ 7-4　你手指著天空，和朋友談天氣：

> How about this weather?
> We really lucked out.
> What a beautiful day!

▶ 7-5　要過十字路口時，你和你朋友說：

> We need to cross.
> Let's cross the street.
> Let's get to the other side.

▶ 7-6　不管你的朋友有沒有闖紅燈，你都可以跟他說：

> Don't jaywalk.
> Don't go against the light.
> You'll get hit by a car.

▶7-7 走到公園，你和朋友說：

> Here's a favorite park.
> It's a popular spot.
> It's a super place to unwind.

▶7-8 走到夜市，你和朋友說：

> Here's a great market.
> It's pretty famous.
> It's noted for its bargains.

▶7-9 走到一家名牌店，你和你的朋友說：

> This store is number one.
> It's the top place to shop.
> It's the hottest store in town.

▶7-10 走到路邊的椅子，你和朋友說：

> Let's hang out.
> Let's stick around.
> Let's stay here for a while.

▶7-11 晚上看到車水馬龍的街道，你和朋友說：

> This city is dynamic.
> It's a mix of East and West.
> It's a combination of old and new.

▶7-12 回家路上，你和你朋友說：

> You're a fun person.
> You're great to be with.
> I like being around you.

1. *Let's hit the road.*

Let's hit the road.	我們走吧。
Let's get moving.	我們走吧。
Let's hustle out of here.	讓我們趕快離開這裡吧。
Do you like to walk?	你喜歡走路嗎？
Do you mind walking?	你介意走路嗎？
We'll see more on foot.	我們走路可以看得比較多。
I'm a big walker.	我常走路。
I walk to stay in shape.	我走路是爲了保持健康。
Are your shoes suitable for walking?	你的鞋子適合走路嗎？

** ———————————————

hit the road 出發；動身
move 〔 muv 〕 *v.* 移動；走動；離去；出發
get moving 動身   hustle 〔ˈhʌsl̩ 〕 *v.* 趕快；急速行進
mind 〔 maɪnd 〕 *v.* 介意   *on foot* 步行
walker 〔ˈwɔkɚ 〕 *n.* 步行者；常散步的人
stay 〔 ste 〕 *v.* 保持
shape 〔 ʃep 〕 *n.* (健康等的) 狀態；情況
in shape 健康的   shoes 〔 ʃuz 〕 *n. pl.* 鞋子
suitable 〔ˈsutəbl̩ 〕 *adj.* 適合的

BOOK 7

2. Hold it a second.

Oops!	哎喲！
Hold it a second.	等一下。
I almost forgot.	我差點忘記了。
I'm short of cash.	我缺少現金。
I need some bucks.	我需要一些錢。
I need to hit an ATM.	我必須去提款機提款。
You can join me.	你可以和我一起去。
You can wait here.	你可以在這裡等。
It's up to you.	由你決定。

** ————————————

oops〔ups〕*interj.* 噢；哎喲　　*hold it* 等一下
second〔'sɛkənd〕*n.* 秒　　*a second* 一會兒；片刻
short〔ʃɔrt〕*adj.* 缺乏的；不足的　　*be short of* 缺少
cash〔kæʃ〕*n.* 現金　　buck〔bʌk〕*n.* 美元
hit〔hɪt〕*v.* 到達（= *go to*）
ATM 自動櫃員機；自動提款機
　（= *automatic-teller machine*）
join〔dʒɔɪn〕*v.* 加入；和…作伴；和…一起做同樣的事
be up to sb. 由某人決定

3. Thanks for waiting.

Thanks for waiting.	謝謝你等我。
Sorry about that.	很抱歉。
Sorry I took so long.	抱歉，我花費那麼長的時間。
The line was long.	排隊排很長。
It was slower than slow.	非常慢。
It was the line from hell.	排隊排得很長。
I almost lost it.	我差點要生氣。
I almost blew a fuse.	我幾乎要大發脾氣。
I was ready to explode.	我快要大發脾氣。

**　**

take〔tek〕*v.* 花費（時間）　　line〔laɪn〕*n.* 行列

hell〔hɛl〕*n.* 地獄

blow〔blo〕*v.*（保險絲）使燒斷

fuse〔fjuz〕*n.* 保險絲

blow a fuse 燒斷保險絲；大發雷霆

be ready to 快要；就要　　explode〔ɪkˋsplod〕*v.* 爆發

BOOK 7

4. *How about this weather?*

How about this weather?	你覺得這個天氣怎麼樣？
We really lucked out.	我們眞幸運。
What a beautiful day!	多麼好的天氣！
It's not too hot.	不會太熱。
It's not too cold.	不會太冷。
It's just right.	天氣剛剛好。
I hope it holds up.	我希望天氣能保持良好。
Let's cross our fingers.	希望我們有好運氣。
Let's enjoy it while we can.	在我們能夠的時候，享受這個好天氣吧。

** ————————————

weather〔'wɛðə〕*n.* 天氣
luck〔lʌk〕*v.* 逢凶化吉；靠運氣　　*luck out* 運氣好
just right 剛好　　*hold up* 維持；保持良好
cross〔krɔs〕*v.* 使交叉
cross one's fingers 祈求好運

5. We need to cross.

We need to cross.	我們需要過馬路。
Let's cross the street.	我們穿越馬路吧。
Let's get to the other side.	我們過馬路到另外一邊吧。
Heads up.	注意。
Look both ways.	看看兩個方向的來車。
Look before you cross.	在你過馬路以前要看一看。
The traffic is dangerous.	來往的車輛很危險。
It's like a jungle out there.	交通很危險。
You can never be too careful.	你要非常小心。

** ───────────────

cross〔krɔs〕*v.* 橫越　　***get to*** 到達

side〔saɪd〕*n.* 邊　　***heads up*** 注意

way〔we〕*n.* 方向

traffic〔'træfɪk〕*n.* 交通；來往的車輛及行人

dangerous〔'dendʒərəs〕*adj.* 危險的

jungle〔'dʒʌŋgl̩〕*n.* 叢林　　***out there*** 外面；在那邊

can never be too ～　再～也不爲過；越～越好

6. *Don't jaywalk.*

Don't jaywalk.	不要擅自穿越馬路。
Don't go against the light.	不要闖紅燈。
You'll get hit by a car.	你會被車撞到。
Wait on the curb.	在路邊等。
Wait for the green.	等綠燈。
Always use the crosswalk.	一定要使用行人穿越道。
Be alert.	要小心。
Be careful.	要小心。
Use your head to stay safe.	用你的頭腦來保命。

** ———————————————

jaywalk〔'dʒeˌwɔk〕 *v.*（不遵守交通規則）擅自穿越馬路
go against 違反
light〔laɪt〕 *n.* 交通號誌燈（= *traffic light*）
hit〔hɪt〕 *v.* 撞　　curb〔kɝb〕 *n.*（人行道旁的）邊欄或邊石
green〔grin〕 *n.* 綠色信號燈
crosswalk〔'krɔsˌwɔk〕 *n.* 行人穿越道
alert〔ə'lɝt〕 *adj.* 留心的；警覺的　　head〔hɛd〕 *n.* 頭腦
use one's head 運用頭腦思考　　stay〔ste〕 *v.* 保持

7. *Here's a favorite park.*

Here's a favorite park.	這裡是大家所喜愛的公園。
It's a popular spot.	它是一個大家喜歡的地方。
It's a super place to unwind.	這是讓人放鬆的超好地方。
This park is alive.	這個公園生氣勃勃。
It's full of energy.	它充滿了活力。
It's the place to be.	它是該去的地方。
You can see families enjoying themselves.	你可以看到很多家庭玩得很愉快。
You can see people exercising.	你可以看到人們在運動。
Mornings and evenings are best.	早晨和晚上最好。

** ─────────────

favorite〔'fevərɪt〕*adj.* 特別受喜愛的；最喜愛的
popular〔'pɑpjələ〕*adj.* 受歡迎的
spot〔spɑt〕*n.* 地點；場所
super〔'supə〕*adj.* 極好的；超級的
unwind〔ʌn'waɪnd〕*v.* 放鬆（= *relax*）
alive〔ə'laɪv〕*adj.* 熱鬧的；有活力的；生氣勃勃的
be full of 充滿   energy〔'ɛnədʒɪ〕*n.* 活力
enjoy oneself 玩得愉快   exercise〔'ɛksə,saɪz〕*v.* 運動

BOOK 7

8. *Here's a great market.*

Here's a great market.	這裡有一個很棒的市場。
It's pretty famous.	它非常有名。
It's noted for its bargains.	那裡的東西出名的便宜。
You should haggle.	你應該討價還價。
You should negotiate.	你應該討價還價。
You must talk the price down.	你必須殺價。
The sellers are pros.	這些人很會賣東西。
They'll steal you blind.	他們要騙你太容易了。
They'll rip you off without blinking an eye.	他們敲你竹槓時，面不改色。

** ――――――――――――――――――

market〔'mɑrkɪt〕*n.* 市場　　pretty〔'prɪtɪ〕*adv.* 非常
famous〔'feməs〕*adj.* 有名的　　noted〔'notɪd〕*adj.* 有名的
be noted for 以～有名　　bargain〔'bɑrgɪn〕*n.* 便宜貨
haggle〔'hægl̩〕*v.* 討價還價
negotiate〔nɪ'goʃɪ,et〕*v.* 談判；交涉；討價還價
seller〔'sɛlɚ〕*n.* 銷售者；賣方
pro〔pro〕*n.* 專家 (= *expert*)
steal〔stil〕*v.* 偷；不知不覺中取走
blind〔blaɪnd〕*adj.* 瞎的　*adv.* 盲目地
rip *sb*. **off** 敲某人竹槓　　blink〔blɪŋk〕*v.* 眨（眼）

9.   *This store is number one*.

This store is number one.	這家商店最好。
It's the top place to shop.	這裡是買東西最好的地方。
It's the hottest store in town.	它是城裡最受歡迎的店。
They have the best stuff.	他們有最好的東西。
They have the top brands.	他們有賣最好的品牌。
There's always a sale going on.	總是有東西在特價出售。
This store is unbelievable.	這家店令人難以相信。
They've got everything you need.	他們有你所需要的每樣東西。
They have it all from A to Z.	他們什麼都有。

** ——————————————————————

number one 最好的；一流的
top 〔 tɑp 〕*adj.* 最高級的；最優良的
shop 〔 ʃɑp 〕*v.* 在商店購物
hot 〔 hɑt 〕*adj.* 熱門的；受歡迎的   *in town* 在城裡
stuff 〔 stʌf 〕*n.* 東西   brand 〔 brænd 〕*n.* 品牌
sale 〔 sel 〕*n.* 特價；拍賣   *go on* 進行
unbelievable 〔ˌʌnbəˋlivəbḷ 〕*adj.* 令人無法相信的
they've got 他們有   *from A to Z* 從頭到尾；完全地

10. Let's hang out.

Let's hang out.	我們待在這裡吧。
Let's stick around.	我們待在附近吧。
Let's stay here for a while.	我們在這裡待一會兒吧。
We can relax.	我們可以放輕鬆。
We can chill out.	我們可以輕鬆一下。
We can mellow out.	我們可以輕鬆一下。
Take a load off.	坐下來休息一下。
Take a little rest.	休息一會兒。
We can watch the crowd.	我們可以看人群走來走去。

** ─────────────────

hang out 閒蕩；消磨時間　　*stick around* 逗留；等待
for a while 一會兒　　relax〔rɪˈlæks〕*v.* 放鬆
chill〔tʃɪl〕*v.* 變冷　　*chill out* 放鬆一下
mellow〔ˈmɛlo〕*v.* 變柔和　　*mellow out* 放鬆一下
load〔lod〕*n.* 負擔　　*take a load off* 坐下來休息一下
take a rest 休息一下　　crowd〔kraud〕*n.* 人群

11. This city is dynamic.

This city is dynamic.	這個城市充滿活力。
It's a mix of East and West.	它是東、西方的混合。
It's a combination of old and new.	它是新和舊的結合。
This city never sleeps.	這個城市從不睡覺。
It's a 24/7 city.	這個城市是不夜城,全年無休。
It's always on the go.	它總是很忙碌。
This city has it all.	這個城市什麼都有。
To see it is to like it.	看到它,你就會喜歡它。
To live here is to love it.	住在這裡,你就會愛上它。

**————————————

dynamic〔daɪ'næmɪk〕*adj.* 動態的;充滿活力的
mix〔mɪks〕*n.* 混合   East〔ist〕*n.* 東方(各國)
West〔wɛst〕*n.* 西洋;歐美(各國)
combination〔ˌkɑmbə'neʃən〕*n.* 結合
old〔old〕*n.* 舊事物   new〔nju〕*n.* 新事物
24/7 唸成 twenty-four seven,指「一星期七天,二十四
　　小時不停」,也就是「全年無休」。
on the go 很忙碌   *has it all* 什麼都有

BOOK 7

12. *You're a fun person*.

You're a fun person.	和你在一起很愉快。
You're great to be with.	和你在一起很棒。
I like being around you.	我喜歡和你在一起。
You're easygoing.	你很隨和。
You're easy to please.	你很容易滿意。
You have a nice personality.	你的個性很好。
I like your spirit.	我欣賞你的活力。
You're full of life.	你很有活力。
You're always a good time.	和你在一起總是很愉快。

**

fun〔fʌn〕*adj.* 好玩的；有趣的；令人愉快的
great〔gret〕*adj.* 很棒的
around〔ə'raʊnd〕*prep.* 在…周圍
easygoing〔'izɪ'goɪŋ〕*adj.* 脾氣隨和的；隨遇而安的
please〔pliz〕*v.* 取悅；使滿意
personality〔͵pɝsṇ'ælətɪ〕*n.* 個性
spirit〔'spɪrɪt〕*n.* 精神；活力
be full of 充滿   life〔laɪf〕*n.* 活力

「一口氣背會話」經 BOOK 7

唸英文要像唸經一樣，每天大聲唸，從起床到睡覺，唸得比看得快，最後不看也會唸，養成習慣後，你會全身舒爽，你試試看，奇妙無比。

1. *Let's* hit the road.
   Let's get moving.
   Let's hustle out of here.

   Do you like to walk?
   Do you mind walking?
   We'll see more on foot.

   I'm a big walker.
   I walk to stay in shape.
   Are your shoes suitable for walking?

2. Oops!
   Hold it a second.
   I almost forgot.

   I'm short of cash.
   I need some bucks.
   I need to hit an ATM.

   You can join me.
   You can wait here.
   It's up to you.

3. Thanks for waiting.
   Sorry about that.
   Sorry I took so long.

   The line was long.
   It was slower than slow.
   It was the line from hell.

   I almost lost it.
   I almost blew a fuse.
   I was ready to explode.

4. How about this weather?
   We really lucked out.
   What a beautiful day!

   It's not too hot.
   It's not too cold.
   It's just right.

   I hope it holds up.
   Let's cross our fingers.
   Let's enjoy it while we can.

5. We need to cross.
   Let's cross the street.
   Let's get to the other side.

   Heads up.
   Look both ways.
   Look before you cross.

   The traffic is dangerous.
   It's like a jungle out there.
   You can never be too careful.

6. *Don't* jaywalk.
   Don't go against the light.
   You'll get hit by a car.

   Wait on the curb.
   Wait for the green.
   Always use the crosswalk.

   Be alert.
   Be careful.
   Use your head to stay safe.

7. Here's a favorite park.
   It's a popular spot.
   It's a super place to unwind.

   This park is alive.
   It's full of energy.
   It's the place to be.

   You can see families enjoying
      themselves.
   You can see people exercising.
   Mornings and evenings are best.

8. Here's a great market.
   It's pretty famous.
   It's noted for its bargains.

   You should haggle.
   You should negotiate.
   You must talk the price down.

   The sellers are pros.
   They'll steal you blind.
   They'll rip you off without
      blinking an eye.

9. This store is number one.
   It's the top place to shop.
   It's the hottest store in town.

   They have the best stuff.
   They have the top brands.
   There's always a sale going on.

   This store is unbelievable.
   They've got everything you need.
   They have it all from A to Z.

10. *Let's* hang out.
    Let's stick around.
    Let's stay here for a while.

    We can relax.
    We can chill out.
    We can mellow out.

    Take a load off.
    Take a little rest.
    We can watch the crowd.

11. This city is dynamic.
    It's a mix of East and West.
    It's a combination of old and new.

    This city never sleeps.
    It's a 24/7 city.
    It's always on the go.

    This city has it all.
    To see it is to like it.
    To live here is to love it.

12. *You're* a fun person.
    You're great to be with.
    I like being around you.

    You're easygoing.
    You're easy to please.
    You have a nice personality.

    I like your spirit.
    You're full of life.
    You're always a good time.

BOOK 8 和外國人搭訕

▶8-1 看到一個外國人坐在椅子上，旁邊有空位，你可以說：

> Is this seat taken?
> Is anyone sitting here?
> Mind if I sit down?

▶8-2 坐在椅子上，可和外國人繼續說：

> How are you?
> How's it going?
> Having a good day?

▶8-3 問旁邊的外國人時間：

> Excuse me, please.
> What time is it?
> Do you have the time?

▶8-4 可以和外國人聊聊天氣：

> What a rotten day!
> What a terrible day!
> Pretty awful, huh?

▶8-5 看到外國人好像需要幫忙，就可說：

> Need any help?
> Need a hand?
> Can I do anything for you?

▶8-5 問外國人你書中不懂的地方：

> Can I ask a favor?
> Can you spare a minute?
> Can you help me with this?
>
> What does this mean?

►8-7 可以學美國人一樣，讚美別人的服裝：

I like your shirt!
That's your color!
That looks great on you!

►8-8 感覺外國人有點面熟時說：

You look familiar.
You got me thinking.
Have we met before?

►8-9 想得到一些資訊，就問他：

Can I ask you a question?
I need information.
I could use some advice.

►8-10 想和外國人進一步聊天時說：

Mind if I join you?
Care for some company?
I don't want to intrude.

►8-11 想問他的身份時，就可說：

I bet you're a student.
Where do you study?
What grade are you in?

►8-12 走在街上，問路怎麼走：

I'm a little lost.
I need directions.
Can you set me straight?

1. *Is this seat taken?*

Is this seat taken?	這個位子有人坐嗎？
Is anyone sitting here?	有沒有人坐這裡？
Mind if I sit down?	你介不介意我坐在這裡？
Is it OK?	可以嗎？
Is it all right?	好嗎？
Do you mind?	你介意嗎？
What a crowd!	這麼多人！
This place is packed!	這個地方很擁擠！
Seats are going fast!	座位很快就不見了！

** ————————————————

seat〔sit〕*n.* 座位　　***take a seat*** 坐下
mind〔maɪnd〕*v.* 介意
all right 沒問題的；好的
crowd〔kraʊd〕*n.* 人群
packed〔pækt〕*adj.* 擠滿人的　　go〔go〕*v.* 消失

2. *How are you?*

How are you?	你好嗎？
How's it going?	情況進展得如何？
Having a good day?	你今天愉快嗎？
I haven't seen you before.	我以前沒看過你。
Are you new in town?	你是不是剛來這裡的？
Are you working or visiting here?	你是在這裡工作，還是來這裡玩？
How long have you been here?	你來這裡多久了？
How long are you staying?	你要待多久？
Do you like it here?	你喜不喜歡這裡？

**

go〔go〕*v.* 進展　　new〔nju〕*adj.* 新來的
in town 在城裡；在這裡（= *here*）
visit〔'vɪzɪt〕*v.* 遊覽　　stay〔ste〕*v.* 停留

3. *What time is it?*

Excuse me, please.	對不起，拜託。
What time is it?	現在幾點？
Do you have the time?	你知不知道現在幾點？
I forgot my watch.	我忘記戴手錶。
I've lost track of time.	我不知道時間。
I have no idea what time it is.	我不知道現在幾點。
I appreciate it.	我很感激你。
I thank you so much.	我非常感謝你。
You're very kind.	你真好心。

**

track〔træk〕*n.* 蹤跡
lose track of 失去…的蹤跡；不知道
have no idea 不知道
appreciate〔ə'priʃɪ,et〕*v.* 感激
kind〔kaɪnd〕*adj.* 親切的；好心的

4. What a rotten day!

What a rotten day!	好爛的天氣！
What a terrible day!	天氣真糟糕！
Pretty awful, huh?	天氣很糟糕，不是嗎？
It's crummy.	真糟糕。
It's lousy.	天氣很糟糕。
This really stinks.	天氣真的很糟糕。
It's gloomy.	天氣很陰沈。
It's depressing.	它令人沮喪。
This really gets me down.	這種天氣真使我難受。

** ────────────────────

rotten〔ˈrɑtn̩〕*adj.* 腐爛的；令人討厭的；壞的
terrible〔ˈtɛrəbl̩〕*adj.* 可怕的；很糟糕的
pretty〔ˈprɪtɪ〕*adv.* 非常　awful〔ˈɔfl̩〕*adj.* 可怕的；糟糕的
crummy〔ˈkrʌmɪ〕*adj.* 無價值的；低劣的；糟糕的
lousy〔ˈlaʊzɪ〕*adj.* 糟糕的
stink〔stɪŋk〕*v.* 發出惡臭；很糟糕
gloomy〔ˈglumɪ〕*adj.* 陰暗的；陰沈的
depressing〔dɪˈprɛsɪŋ〕*adj.* 令人沮喪的
down〔daʊn〕*adj.* 沮喪的　*get sb. down* 使某人沮喪

5. *Need any help?*

Need any help?	需要任何幫助嗎？
Need a hand?	需要幫助嗎？
Can I do anything for you?	我能爲你做些什麼事嗎？
Any problem?	有任何問題嗎？
Anything wrong?	有什麼不對勁嗎？
Anything I can do?	有什麼我能做的嗎？
I'd like to help.	我很願意幫忙。
I don't mind a bit.	我一點也不介意。
I'd be happy to help.	我會很高興幫忙。

** —————————————

hand〔hænd〕*n.* 手；幫助
problem〔'prɑbləm〕*n.* 問題
wrong〔rɔŋ〕*adj.* 不對勁的；有問題的
mind〔maɪnd〕*v.* 介意
a bit 一點   *not…a bit* 一點也不

6. *Can I ask a favor?*

Can I ask a favor?	能不能請你幫個忙？
Can you spare a minute?	你能不能抽出一點時間？
Can you help me with this?	你能不能幫我做這件事？
What does this mean?	這是什麼意思？
What's this about?	這是什麼意思？
I can't figure this out.	我不了解這個。
I don't want to disturb you.	我不想要打擾你。
I hope I'm not bothering you.	我希望我沒打擾到你。
If you're busy, I understand.	如果你忙的話，我會了解的。

** ─────────────────

favor〔ˈfevə〕*n.* 恩惠；幫忙
ask sb. a favor 請某人幫忙
spare〔spɛr〕*v.* 抽出（時間）　　minute〔ˈmɪnɪt〕*n.* 片刻
help sb. with sth. 幫助某人做某事
mean〔min〕*v.* 意思是　　*figure out* 了解
disturb〔dɪˈstɝb〕*v.* 打擾　　bother〔ˈbɑðə〕*v.* 打擾

7. *I like your shirt!*

I like your shirt!	我喜歡你的襯衫！
That's your color!	那個顏色最適合你！
That looks great on you!	你穿那件衣服很好看！
It's a nice style.	它的款式很好看。
It caught my eye.	它讓我想不看都不行。
It's just what I'm looking for.	它正是我在找的。
Where did you get it?	你在哪裡買的？
When did you buy it?	你什麼時候買的？
Mind if I ask the price?	你介意我問價錢嗎？

**

shirt〔ʃɝt〕*n.* 襯衫

great〔gret〕*adj.* 極美的；極好的；很棒的

style〔staɪl〕*n.* 風格；款式　　eye〔aɪ〕*n.* 目光；注意

***catch** one's eye* 引起某人的注意

get〔gɛt〕*v.* 得到；買　　mind〔maɪnd〕*v.* 介意

price〔praɪs〕*n.* 價格

8. *You look familiar.*

You look familiar.	你看起來很面熟。
You got me thinking.	你讓我想想看。
Have we met before?	我們以前見過面嗎？
I feel like I know you.	我覺得我好像認識你。
I feel like I've seen you	我覺得我好像在哪裡看過
somewhere.	你。
I can't recall your name.	我想不起你的名字。
I'm Pat Smith.	我是派特・史密斯。
Everyone calls me Pat.	大家都叫我派特。
May I ask your name?	能不能請問你叫什麼名字？

**

familiar〔fəˈmɪljə〕*adj.* 熟悉的
get〔gɛt〕*v.* 使得　　think〔θɪŋk〕*v.* 想；思考
meet〔mit〕*v.* 遇到；與～見面　*feel like* 覺得好像
somewhere〔ˈsʌmˌhwɛr〕*adv.* 在某處
recall〔rɪˈkɔl〕*v.* 想起

9. Can I ask you a question?

Can I ask you a question?	我能問你一個問題嗎？
I need information.	我需要一些資訊。
I could use some advice.	我有點想要一些建議。
I just got here.	我剛到這裡。
It's my first time.	這是我的第一次。
I don't know my way around.	我對這個地方不熟悉。
What's worth a look?	什麼值得看？
What's interesting to see?	有什麼有趣的東西可以看？
Anything special or famous nearby?	附近有沒有什麼特別的或有名的東西？

** ——————————

information〔͵ɪnfɚˋmeʃən〕*n.* 消息；資訊
could use 有點想要　　advice〔ədˋvaɪs〕*n.* 忠告；建議
just〔dʒʌst〕*adv.* 剛剛　　get〔gɛt〕*v.* 到達
around〔əˋraʊnd〕*adv.* 在周圍；在附近
know one's way around 對（某處的）地理很清楚；熟知情況
worth〔wɝθ〕*adj.* 值得的　　look〔lʊk〕*n.* 看
interesting〔ˋɪntrɪstɪŋ〕*adj.* 有趣的
famous〔ˋfeməs〕*adj.* 有名的
nearby〔ˋnɪrˋbaɪ〕*adv.* 在附近

10. Mind if I join you?

Mind if I join you?	介不介意我和你在一起？
Care for some company?	你要不要人陪？
I don't want to intrude.	我不想要打擾。
*I'*m not doing anything.	我沒有事情做。
*I'*d welcome the conversation.	我歡迎你和我說話。
It would make my day.	它會使我今天很高興。
Let's have a chat.	我們聊聊天吧。
Let's shoot the breeze.	我們聊聊吧。
Ask me anything you like.	問我任何你喜歡問的事。

**

join〔dʒɔɪn〕*v.* 參加；和…在一起　　*care for* 想要；喜歡
company〔'kʌmpənɪ〕*n.* 公司；陪伴
intrude〔ɪn'trud〕*v.* 干擾；打擾
welcome〔'wɛlkəm〕*v.* 歡迎；愉快地接受
make one's day 使某人（當日）非常高興
chat〔tʃæt〕*n.* 聊天　　shoot〔ʃut〕*v.* 射擊
breeze〔briz〕*n.* 微風　　*shoot the breeze* 聊天

BOOK 8

11. I bet you're a student.

I bet you're a student.	我想你一定是個學生吧。
Where do you study?	你在哪裡讀書？
What grade are you in?	你是幾年級學生？
How's your school?	你的學校怎麼樣？
How do you like it?	你覺得它怎麼樣？
Is it tough or easy?	它是難讀還是容易讀？
Do you like your teachers?	你喜不喜歡你的老師？
Do you get lots of homework?	你有沒有很多功課要做？
What's your favorite class?	你最喜歡上什麼課？

** ─────────────

bet〔bɛt〕*v.* 打賭；確信　　*I bet* 我敢打賭；我確信
grade〔gred〕*n.* 年級　　tough〔tʌf〕*adj.* 困難的
easy〔'izɪ〕*adj.* 容易的；輕鬆的
favorite〔'fevərɪt〕*adj.* 最喜愛的

12. *I'm a little lost.*

I'm a little lost.	我有點迷路。
I need some directions.	我需要你告訴我一下怎麼走。
Can you set me straight?	你能不能告訴我正確的路？
Where's the metro?	地下鐵在哪裡？
Which way is it?	它是在哪個方向？
How do I get there from here?	我如何從這裡到那裡？
How close am I?	離我有多近？
How far away is it?	它有多遠？
Thank you so much for your time.	非常感謝你的時間。

** ─────────────────

lost〔lɔst〕*adj.* 迷路的
direction〔dəˈrɛkʃən〕*n.* 方向；指引
set〔sɛt〕*v.* 使（成某狀態）
straight〔stret〕*adj.* 直的；正確的
set sb. straight 讓某人了解　　metro〔ˈmɛtro〕*n.* 地下鐵
way〔we〕*n.* 方向　　get〔gɛt〕*v.* 到達
close〔klos〕*adj.* 接近的　　*far away* 遙遠

唸英文要像唸經一樣，每天大聲唸，從起床到睡覺，唸得比看得快，最後不看也會唸，養成習慣後，你會全身舒爽，你試試看，奇妙無比。

1. *Is* this seat taken?
   Is anyone sitting here?
   Mind if I sit down?

   Is it OK?
   Is it all right?
   Do you mind?

   What a crowd!
   This place is packed!
   Seats are going fast!

2. *How* are you?
   How's it going?
   Having a good day?

   I haven't seen you before.
   Are you new in town?
   Are you working or visiting here?

   How long have you been here?
   How long are you staying?
   Do you like it here?

3. Excuse me, please.
   What time is it?
   Do you have the time?

   I forgot my watch.
   I've lost track of time.
   I have no idea what time it is.

   I appreciate it.
   I thank you so much.
   You're very kind.

4. *What a* rotten day!
   What a terrible day!
   Pretty awful, huh?

   It's crummy.
   It's lousy.
   This really stinks.

   It's gloomy.
   It's depressing.
   This really gets me down.

5. *Need* any help?
   Need a hand?
   Can I do anything for you?

   Any problem?
   Anything wrong?
   Anything I can do?

   I'd like to help.
   I don't mind a bit.
   I'd be happy to help.

6. Can I ask a favor?
   Can you spare a minute?
   Can you help me with this?

   What does this mean?
   What's this about?
   I can't figure this out.

   I don't want to disturb you.
   I hope I'm not bothering you.
   If you're busy, I understand.

7. I like your shirt!
   That's your color!
   That looks great on you!

   It's a nice style.
   It caught my eye.
   It's just what I'm looking for.

   Where did you get it?
   When did you buy it?
   Mind if I ask the price?

8. *You* look familiar.
   You got me thinking.
   Have we met before?

   I feel like I know you.
   I feel like I've seen you somewhere.
   I can't recall your name.

   I'm Pat Smith.
   Everyone calls me Pat.
   May I ask your name?

9. Can I ask you a question?
   I need information.
   I could use some advice.

   I just got here.
   It's my first time.
   I don't know my way around.

   What's worth a look?
   What's interesting to see?
   Anything special or famous nearby?

10. Mind if I join you?
    Care for some company?
    I don't want to intrude.

    I'm not doing anything.
    I'd welcome the conversation.
    It would make my day.

    Let's have a chat.
    Let's shoot the breeze.
    Ask me anything you like.

11. I bet you're a student.
    Where do you study?
    What grade are you in?

    How's your school?
    How do you like it?
    Is it tough or easy?

    Do you like your teachers?
    Do you get lots of homework?
    What's your favorite class?

12. *I*'m a little lost.
    I need directions.
    Can you set me straight?

    Where's the metro?
    Which way is it?
    How do I get there from here?

    How close am I?
    How far away is it?
    Thank you so much for your tim

BOOK 9 上班族的一天

▶9-1 早上一進辦公室，看到同事就可說：

> Good morning.
> How was your night?
> Did you sleep well?

▶9-2 當你打電話找人的時候，你就可以說：

> I'm calling for Dale.
> My name is Chris.
> May I speak to him, please?

▶9-3 當公司快要開會的時候，你可以跟同事說：

> We have a meeting.
> We have to be there.
> We can't be late.

▶9-4 當你要加班的時候，就可以說：

> I'm working overtime.
> I'm staying late.
> I have too much to do.

▶9-5 當你要和別人約會時，你就可說：

> Let's make an appointment.
> Let's set up a time.
> We need to get together.

▶9-6 當你要取消和別人的約會，你就可以說：

> I have bad news.
> I have to cancel.
> I can't make it.

▶9-7 當你外出回到辦公室，就可以問你的同事：

Any messages for me?
Any calls to return?
What needs to be done?

▶9-8 當你想要請假，就可以跟主管說：

I have a favor to ask.
I need some time off.
I have something important to do.

▶9-9 當你想要加薪時，就可以說：

Do you have a minute?
Can I speak with you?
Can we have a word in private?

▶9-10 到了公司休息時間，你就可以說：

It's break time.
How about a drink?
How about some coffee or tea?

▶9-11 當你接到電話時，你就可以說：

How may I help you?
How may I direct your call?
What can I do for you?

▶9-12 下班的時候，你就可以跟同事說：

It's quitting-time.
It's time to get off.
It's time to go home.

1. How was your night?

Good morning.	早安。
How was your night?	你昨晚睡得如何？
Did you sleep well?	你睡得好不好？
How's your schedule?	你今天有什麼安排？
How's your day today?	你今天忙不忙？
Are you pretty busy?	你是不是相當忙？
I have a lot to do.	我有很多事要做。
I have a full day.	我整天都排得滿滿的。
It's gonna be a long day.	今天將會很忙。

** ————————————

schedule〔'skɛdʒul〕*n.* 時間表；計劃（表）；日程安排
pretty〔'prɪtɪ〕*adv.* 很；非常；相當
full〔fʊl〕*adj.* 排得滿滿的
gonna〔'gɔnə〕（= *going to*）

2. I'm calling for Dale.

I'm calling for Dale.	我要找戴爾。
My name is Chris.	我的名字是克里斯。
May I speak to him, please?	請問我可以和他說話嗎？
Is he in?	他在不在？
Is he available?	他有沒有空？
Is now a good time?	現在的時間恰不恰當？
Can I leave a message?	我能不能留個話？
Can you take a message?	你能不能幫我傳個話？
Please tell him to call me back.	請告訴他回我電話。

**

Dale〔del〕*n.* 戴爾；黛爾
Chris〔krɪs〕*n.* 克里斯；克麗絲
in〔ɪn〕*adv.* 在家；在辦公室
available〔əˈveləbḷ〕*adj.* 有空的　　good〔gʊd〕*adj.* 恰當的
leave〔liv〕*v.* 留下　　message〔ˈmɛsɪdʒ〕*n.* 訊息；留言
leave a message 留個話　　***take a message*** 記錄留言
call sb. back 回電話給某人

3. *We have a meeting.*

We have a meeting.	我們有會要開。
We have to be there.	我們必須到那裡。
We can't be late.	我們不能遲到。
It's starting soon.	快要開始了。
It's almost time.	時間差不多了。
We have to hurry.	我們必須趕快。
Let's leave now.	我們現在走吧。
Let's go together.	我們一起去吧。
There is no time to lose.	沒時間可浪費了。

** ─────────────────────

meeting〔'mitɪŋ〕*n.* 會議
have a meeting 開一次會議
late〔let〕*adj.* 遲到的
hurry〔'hɝɪ〕*v.* 趕快　　lose〔luz〕*v.* 浪費

BOOK 9

4. I'm working overtime.

I'm working overtime.	我要加班。
I'm staying late.	我會待得晚一點。
I have too much to do.	我有太多工作要做。
This work is due.	這個工作必須要完成。
This has to be done.	這個必須要做完。
The deadline is coming up.	截止時間就要到了。
I'm behind.	我落後了。
I have to catch up.	我必須趕上。
*I'*d like to get ahead.	我要超前。

** ————————

overtime〔'ovɚ,taɪm〕*adv.* 超出時間地;加班地
work overtime 加班　　stay〔ste〕*v.* 停留
late〔let〕*adv.* (比適當時刻)晚　　due〔dju〕*adj.* 到期的
deadline〔'dɛd,laɪn〕*n.* 截止時間;最後期限
behind〔bɪ'haɪnd〕*adv.* 落在後面　　***catch up*** 趕上
get ahead 領先;超前

5. *Let's make an appointment.*

Let's make an appointment.	我們約個時間見面吧。
Let's set up a time.	我們安排一個時間吧。
We need to get together.	我們需要見面。
When can we meet?	我們什麼時候可以見面？
When is it convenient?	什麼時間方便？
I'll leave it up to you.	我將留給你決定。
How about tomorrow morning at nine?	明天早上九點如何？
How does that sound?	你覺得如何？
Do you have anything planned?	你有沒有任何計劃？

**

appointment 〔 ə'pɔɪntmənt 〕 *n.* 約會；約定
set up 安排　　*get together* 見面；會面
up to 由…決定的　　sound 〔 saʊnd 〕 *v.* 聽起來
planned 〔 plænd 〕 *adj.* 計劃好的

BOOK 9

6. *I have to cancel*.

I have bad news.	我有壞消息。
I have to cancel.	我必須取消約會。
I can't make it.	我沒辦法辦到。
Something has come up.	有事情發生了。
Can we reschedule?	我們可不可以重新訂時間？
Can we meet another time?	我們能不能另外找一個時間見面？
You tell me.	由你決定。
You pick the time.	你選擇時間。
I'll work around your schedule.	我會根據你的時間來安排我的時間。

**─────────

news〔njuz〕*n.* 消息　　cancel〔'kænsḷ〕*v.* 取消；取消約會
make it 成功；辦到　　*come up* 發生
reschedule〔ri'skɛdʒul〕*v.* 重新排定…的時間
meet〔mit〕*v.* 會面；見面　　pick〔pɪk〕*v.* 挑選；選擇
around〔ə'raund〕*prep.* 以…為中心；根據
schedule〔'skɛdʒul〕*n.* 時間表

BOOK 9

7. *Any messages for me?*

Any messages for me?	有沒有人留話給我？
Any calls to return?	有沒有電話要回？
What needs to be done?	有什麼需要做的？
Could you check this over?	你能不能幫我檢查看看？
Could you check for mistakes?	你能不能看看有沒有錯誤？
Proofread this for me.	幫我校對這個。
Please type this up.	請把這個打好。
Please print out a copy.	請印一份出來。
I need to fax it right away.	我需要把它立刻傳眞出去。

** ———————————

message〔ˈmɛsɪdʒ〕*n.* 訊息；留言　　call〔kɔl〕*n.* 電話
return〔rɪˈtɜn〕*v.* 回（電話）　　*check over* 檢查
proofread〔ˈprufˌrid〕*v.* 校對　　type〔taɪp〕*v.* 打字
print out 印出　　copy〔ˈkɑpɪ〕*n.* 一份
fax〔fæks〕*v.* 傳眞　　*right away* 立刻

8. *I need some time off*.

I have a favor to ask.	我要請你幫個忙。
I need some time off.	我需要一些時間休息。
I have something important to do.	我有一些重要的事情要做。
Can I take a leave of absence?	我可不可以請假？
Can I take a day off ?	我可不可以請一天假？
Would this Friday be OK?	這個星期五可以嗎？
Sorry for the trouble.	很抱歉造成你的麻煩。
I'll work extra hours next week.	我下星期會增加工作時間。
I promise I'll make it up.	我保證我會補回來。

** ───────────

favor〔'fevɚ〕*n.* 恩惠；幫忙　　off〔ɔf〕*adv.* 不工作；休息
leave〔liv〕*n.* 休假；准許　　absence〔'æbsn̩s〕*n.* 缺席
take a leave of absence 請假【通常是較長時間的假】
take a day off 請一天假　　trouble〔'trʌbl̩〕*n.* 麻煩；打擾
extra〔'ɛkstrə〕*adj.* 額外的　　hours〔aurz〕*n. pl.* 時間
promise〔'pramɪs〕*v.* 保證　　*make up* 補足；彌補；補償

9. *I'd like some feedback.*

Do you have a minute?	你有沒有一點時間？
Can I speak with you?	我可不可以和你說話？
Can we have a word in private?	我們可不可以私下談一談？
I'd like some feedback.	我想要一些意見。
How's my performance?	我的表現如何？
How am I doing so far?	到目前為止我的表現如何？
I want to get better.	我想要變得更好。
Please give me some input.	請給我一些建議。
Please tell me what you think.	請告訴我你的看法如何。

**────────────

minute〔'mɪnɪt〕*n.* 分鐘；片刻；一會兒
have a word 說一兩句話　　*in private* 私下地；祕密地
feedback〔'fid,bæk〕*n.* 反應；反饋意見
performance〔pɚ'fɔrməns〕*n.* 表現
do〔du〕*v.* 表現　　*so far* 到目前為止
input〔'ɪn,pʊt〕*n.* 訊息；評論；建議

10. It's break time.

It's break time.	休息時間到了。
How about a drink?	喝杯飲料如何？
How about some coffee or tea?	喝些咖啡或茶如何？
What's new?	你好嗎？
What's the latest?	有什麼最新消息？
What have you been up to?	你最近在忙些什麼？
How's your family?	你的家人好嗎？
How's your workload?	你的工作有多忙？
Are you handling everything OK?	你是不是每件事情都處理得很好？

**

break〔brek〕*n.* 休息　　***break time*** 休息時間
drink〔drɪŋk〕*n.* 飲料；飲料的一份或一杯
latest〔'letɪst〕*adj.* 最新的　　***be up to*** 忙於
family〔'fæməlɪ〕*n.* 家人
workload〔'wɜk‚lod〕*n.* 工作（量）；工作負擔
handle〔'hændḷ〕*v.* 處理　　OK〔'o'ke〕*adv.* 很好；不錯

11. How may I help you?

How may I help you?	我可以怎樣幫助你？
How may I direct your call?	你要我幫你轉接給誰？
What can I do for you?	我能為你做什麼？
Please hold.	請不要掛斷。
I'll be right with you.	我會立刻回來。
I'll go check and see.	我去看一看。
He can't come to the phone.	他無法來接電話。
He's tied up right now.	他現在很忙。
Please leave your name	請留下你的姓名和電話
and number.	號碼。

** ───────────────

direct〔dəˈrɛkt〕*v.* 指引；指導
direct one's call 轉接某人的電話
hold〔hold〕*v.* 握住；持續   right〔raɪt〕*adv.* 立刻
check〔tʃɛk〕*v.* 檢查；查看
come to the phone 來接電話   *be tied up* 很忙碌
right now 現在   leave〔liv〕*v.* 留下
number〔ˈnʌmbɚ〕*n.* 號碼；電話號碼

12. *It's quitting time.*

It's quitting time.	下班時間到了。
It's time to get off.	下班時間到了。
It's time to go home.	該回家了。
Oh, man!	噢，啊！
I'm really tired out.	我真的累死了。
I'm glad this day is over.	我很高興今天的工作結束了。
We did good.	我們做得好。
We earned our pay.	我們的錢是辛苦賺來的。
We worked our tails off today.	我們今天很努力工作。

** ——————————————

quitting time〔ˈkwɪtɪŋ͵taɪm〕*n.* 下班時間
get off 離開；下班　　oh〔o〕*interj.* 噢；喔；哎喲
man〔mæn〕*interj.* 啊；呀；喂
be tired out 十分疲勞；筋疲力盡
glad〔glæd〕*adj.* 高興的　　over〔ˈovɚ〕*adv.* 完畢；結束
earn〔ɝn〕*v.* 賺（錢）；（經由努力而）獲得
pay〔pe〕*n.* 薪水；報酬　　tail〔tel〕*n.* 尾巴
work one's tail off 非常努力工作（= *work very hard*）

「一口氣背會話」經 BOOK 9

唸英文要像唸經一樣，每天大聲唸，從起床到睡覺，唸得比看得快，最後不看也會唸，養成習慣後，你會全身舒爽，你試試看，奇妙無比。

1. Good morning.
   How was your night?
   Did you sleep well?

   How's your schedule?
   How's your day today?
   Are you pretty busy?

   I have a lot to do.
   I have a full day.
   It's gonna be a long day.

2. I'm calling for Dale.
   My name is Chris.
   May I speak to him, please?

   Is he in?
   Is he available?
   Is now a good time?

   Can I leave a message?
   Can you take a message?
   Please tell him to call me back.

3. *We have* a meeting.
   We have to be there.
   We can't be late.

   It's starting soon.
   It's almost time.
   We have to hurry.

   Let's leave now.
   Let's go together.
   There is no time to lose.

4. *I'm* working overtime.
   I'm staying late.
   I have too much to do.

   This work is due.
   This has to be done.
   The deadline is coming up.

   I'm behind.
   I have to catch up.
   I'd like to get ahead.

5. *Let's* make an appointment.
   Let's set up a time.
   We need to get together.

   When can we meet?
   When is it convenient?
   I'll leave it up to you.

   How about tomorrow morning at nine?
   How does that sound?
   Do you have anything planned?

6. *I have* bad news.
   I have to cancel.
   I can't make it.

   Something has come up.
   Can we reschedule?
   Can we meet another time?

   You tell me.
   You pick the time.
   I'll work around your schedule.

7. *Any* messages for me?
   Any calls to return?
   What needs to be done?

   Could you check this over?
   Could you check for mistakes?
   Proofread this for me.

   Please type this up.
   Please print out a copy.
   I need to fax it right away.

8. *I* have a favor to ask.
   I need some time off.
   I have something important to do.

   Can I take a leave of absence?
   Can I take a day off ?
   Would this Friday be OK?

   Sorry for the trouble.
   *I'*ll work extra hours next week.
   I promise I'll make it up.

9. Do you have a minute?
   Can I speak with you?
   Can we have a word in private?

   I'd like some feedback.
   *How'*s my performance?
   How am I doing so far?

   I want to get better.
   Please give me some input.
   Please tell me what you think.

10. It's break time.
    How about a drink?
    How about some coffee or tea?

    What's new?
    What's the latest?
    What have you been up to?

    How's your family?
    How's your workload?
    Are you handling everything OK?

11. *How may I* help you?
    How may I direct your call?
    What can I do for you?

    Please hold.
    I'll be right with you.
    I'll go check and see.

    He can't come to the phone.
    *He'*s tied up right now.
    Please leave your name and number.

12. *It's* quitting-time.
    It's time to get off.
    It's time to go home.

    Oh, man!
    I'm really tired out.
    I'm glad this day is over.

    We did good.
    We earned our pay.
    We worked our tails off today.

BOOK 10 接待外國賓客

▶10-1 當你想要打電話問你的客人何時到達、坐什麼飛機時，就可說：

> When are you arriving?
> What's the date and time?
> What's your airline and flight number?

▶10-2 當你到達機場，一看到來訪的外國人，你就說：

> Welcome!
> You made it!
> I'm glad you're here.

▶10-3 看到外國客人拿到行李，你就說：

> Let me help.
> Let me carry that.
> I insist.

▶10-4 在汽車裡面，繼續和外國客人說：

> First time here?
> Been here before?
> Have any questions?

▶10-5 聽不懂外國客人講的話時，你就可以說：

> I beg your pardon?
> I didn't catch that.
> What did you say?

▶10-6 當你要帶外國客人去玩，你如果有什麼計劃，就可以說這九句：

> Here's the schedule.
> Take a look.
> See if it's OK.

►10-7 當你要請外國客人吃飯的時候，你就可以說：

How about a meal?
Let me invite you.
I know some good places.

►10-8 在餐廳，要點菜的時候，就可以和外國客人說：

Order anything.
Choose what you like.
Don't worry about the price.

►10-9 看到外國客人身體不舒服，你就可以說：

Are you all right?
Is anything the matter?
Is everything OK?

►10-10 當你打算帶外國客人出去玩的時候，你就可以說：

What are you doing this weekend?
Have any plans?
Want to meet?

►10-11 當你想要和外國客人約時間開車去接他時，你就可以說：

Let's start out early tomorrow.
I'll pick you up at seven-thirty.
I'll be there on time.

►10-12 當你在機場替外國客人送行，要離別時，你就可以說：

I'm sorry you're leaving.
I enjoyed your visit.
I look forward to seeing you again.

1. *When are you arriving?*

When are you arriving?	你什麼時候到達？
What's the date and time?	什麼日期和什麼時間？
What's your airline and flight number?	你搭什麼航空公司，班機號碼是幾號？
What are your plans?	你有什麼計劃？
Do you have reservations?	你有預訂飯店嗎？
Shall I book a room for you?	要不要我幫你預訂房間？
It's fall here.	現在這裡是秋天。
The weather is getting colder.	天氣越來越冷了。
Please pack some warm clothes.	請帶一些保暖的衣服。

** ────────────

arrive〔ə'raɪv〕v. 到達　date〔det〕n. 日期
airline〔'ɛr,laɪn〕n. 航空公司　flight〔flaɪt〕n. 班機
number〔'nʌmbɚ〕n. 號碼
reservation〔,rɛzɚ'veʃən〕n. 預訂
shall〔ʃəl〕aux. 要不要～；～好嗎　book〔buk〕v. 預訂
fall〔fɔl〕n. 秋天　weather〔'wɛðɚ〕n. 天氣
pack〔pæk〕v. 打包　warm〔wɔrm〕adj. 保暖的；暖和的
clothes〔kloz, kloðz〕n. pl. 衣服

BOOK 10

2. You made it!

Welcome!	歡迎！
You made it!	你來了！
I'm glad you're here.	我很高興你來了。
I'm pleased to meet you.	很高興認識你。
I've heard so much about you.	我聽過很多關於你的事。
It's an honor.	很榮幸認識你。
How was your flight?	你這趟飛行如何？
How are you feeling?	你現在感覺如何？
What shall we do first?	你覺得我們應該先做什麼？

** ───────────────────────

welcome〔ˈwɛlkəm〕*interj.* 歡迎
make it 成功；辦到；做到　　glad〔glæd〕*adj.* 高興的
pleased〔plizd〕*adj.* 高興的
meet〔mit〕*v.* 認識；和～見面　　honor〔ˈɑnɚ〕*n.* 光榮的事
flight〔flaɪt〕*n.* 飛行；班機；搭機旅行　　feel〔fil〕*v.* 感覺

3. Shall we go now?

Shall we go now?	我們現在可以走了嗎？
I have a car outside.	我的車在外面。
Please follow me.	請跟我走。
Let me help.	讓我幫你。
Let me carry that.	讓我來拿。
I insist.	我堅持。
Here's the car.	車子在這裡。
Bags go in the trunk.	行李要放在後車廂。
Hop in.	上車。

**

shall 〔ʃəl〕 *aux.* 要不要～；～好嗎

outside 〔'aʊt'saɪd〕 *adv.* 在外面　　follow 〔'falo〕 *v.* 跟隨

carry 〔'kærɪ〕 *v.* 攜帶；拿；提　　insist 〔ɪn'sɪst〕 *v.* 堅持

bag 〔bæg〕 *n.* 手提袋；行李　　***go in*** 被放入

trunk 〔trʌŋk〕 *n.* (汽車) 行李箱；後車廂

hop 〔hap〕 *v.* 跳　　***hop in*** 上車

4. First time here?

First time here?	第一次來這裡嗎？
Been here before?	以前來過這裡嗎？
Have any questions?	有任何問題嗎？
Are you tired at all?	你累不累啊？
Are you hungry or thirsty?	你餓不餓、渴不渴？
If you need anything, let me know.	如果你需要什麼東西，要讓我知道。
How do you like this weather?	你覺得這個天氣怎麼樣？
Is it different?	有沒有什麼不同？
Is it like this back home?	這裡的天氣和你家鄉的相同嗎？

BOOK 10

**────────────────

here〔hɪr〕*adv.* 到這裡　　been〔bɪn, bin〕*v.* 曾到過
tired〔taɪrd〕*adj.* 疲倦的　　*at all* 絲毫；一點
hungry〔'hʌŋgrɪ〕*adj.* 飢餓的　　thirsty〔'θɝstɪ〕*adj.* 口渴的
let〔lɛt〕*v.* 讓　　weather〔'wɛðɚ〕*n.* 天氣
different〔'dɪfrənt〕*adj.* 不同的
back home 在你的家鄉；在你住的地方

5. *I beg your pardon?*

I beg your pardon?	對不起，請再說一遍好嗎？
I didn't catch that.	我沒聽懂。
What did you say?	你說什麼？
Could you repeat that?	你能不能再說一遍？
Could you speak up?	你可以說大聲一點嗎？
Please speak slowly.	請說慢一點。
I don't get it.	我聽不懂你說的話。
What do you mean?	你的意思是什麼？
Please explain it to me.	請解釋給我聽。

BOOK 10

** ————————————

beg〔bɛg〕*v.* 請求　　pardon〔'pɑrdṇ〕*n.* 原諒

catch〔kætʃ〕*v.* 聽懂　　repeat〔rɪ'pit〕*v.* 重複；重說

speak up 大聲說　　get〔gɛt〕*v.* 了解；聽懂

mean〔min〕*v.* 意思是

explain〔ɪk'splen〕*v.* 解釋；說明

6. *Here's the schedule*.

Here's the schedule.	這是行程表。
Take a look.	看一看。
See if it's OK.	看一看是否可以。
*I'*d like your opinion.	我想要你的意見。
I want your approval.	我希望有你的同意。
You can change it if you want.	如果你想改，就可以改。
Let's discuss it.	我們一起討論吧。
Let's go over it.	我們檢查一下吧。
I want everything to be clear.	我想要一切都很清楚。

**————————————

schedule〔'skɛdʒul〕*n.* 行程表
take a look 看一看   if〔ɪf〕*conj.* 是否
I'd like 我想要 (= *I would like* = *I want*)
opinion〔ə'pɪnjən〕*n.* 意見   approval〔ə'pruvḷ〕*n.* 同意
change〔tʃendʒ〕*v.* 改變   discuss〔dɪ'skʌs〕*v.* 討論
go over 查看；檢查   clear〔klɪr〕*adj.* 明確的；清楚的

7. *How about a meal?*

How about a meal?	吃頓飯如何？
Let me invite you.	我想請你。
I know some good places.	我知道一些好地方。
You'll like it.	你會喜歡的。
You'll have fun.	你會很開心。
It'll be a good time.	那將很愉快。
Do you have time?	你有時間嗎？
We won't be gone long.	我們不會離開很久。
You're welcome to join me.	歡迎你和我一起去。

BOOK 10

** ————————————————

How about~? ～如何？   meal〔mil〕*n.* 一餐
invite〔ɪn'vaɪt〕*v.* 邀請
have fun 玩得愉快；開心；高興
a good time 愉快的時光   gone〔gɔn〕*adj.* 離去的
long〔lɔŋ〕*adv.* 長久地；很久地
welcome〔'wɛlkəm〕*adj.* 受歡迎的
join〔dʒɔɪn〕*v.* 參加；加入；和…一起做同樣的事

8. Order anything.

Order anything.	隨便點任何東西。
Choose what you like.	選擇你喜歡的。
Don't worry about the price.	別擔心價錢。
This dish is a house favorite.	這道菜是這個餐廳的招牌菜。
I've had it before.	我以前吃過。
It's very tasty.	它很好吃。
How is it?	你覺得怎麼樣？
Is it good?	好不好吃？
Want some more?	還要再來一些嗎？

BOOK 10

**

order〔'ɔrdɚ〕v. 點（菜）　　choose〔tʃuz〕v. 選擇
dish〔dɪʃ〕n. 菜餚　　***worry about*** 擔心
price〔praɪs〕n. 價錢
favorite〔'fevərɪt〕n. 最受喜愛的人或物
house favorite 招牌菜　　have〔hæv〕v. 吃；喝
tasty〔'testɪ〕adj. 美味的；好吃的

9. Are you all right?

Are you all right?	你沒問題吧？
Is anything the matter?	有什麼不對勁的嗎？
Is everything OK?	一切都還可以吧？
You look a little pale.	你的臉色有點蒼白。
You must be exhausted.	你一定是累壞了。
I bet you're tired.	我想你一定是累了。
Can I get you anything?	我能為你拿任何東西嗎？
Want to take some medicine?	要吃點藥嗎？
Do you want me to take you to the doctor?	你要不要我帶你去看醫生？

** ─────────────────────

all right 沒問題的   *the matter* 不對勁的
pale 〔 pel 〕 *adj.* 蒼白的
exhausted 〔 ɪgˊzɔstɪd 〕 *adj.* 筋疲力盡的
bet 〔 bɛt 〕 *v.* 打賭   *I bet* 我敢說；我相信；我認為；我想
tired 〔 taɪrd 〕 *adj.* 疲倦的   get 〔 gɛt 〕 *v.* 去拿來
take 〔 tek 〕 *v.* 吃（藥）   medicine 〔ˊmɛdəsn 〕 *n.* 藥

10. **Have any plans?**

What are you doing this weekend?	這個週末你打算做什麼？
Have any plans?	有任何計劃嗎？
Want to meet?	想要見面聚一聚嗎？
I have some free time.	我有一些空閒時間。
Want to go sightseeing?	想要去觀光嗎？
Want to do something fun?	想做一些好玩的事嗎？
Let me be your guide.	讓我當你的導遊。
What are your interests?	你的興趣是什麼？
What do you want to do?	你想要做什麼？

**───────────

weekend〔'wik'ɛnd〕*n.* 週末
plan〔plæn〕*n.* 計劃　　meet〔mit〕*v.* 見面
free〔fri〕*adj.* 空閒的；有空的　　***free time*** 空閒時間
sightsee〔'saɪt,si〕*v.* 觀光【sightseeing 在此是動名詞】
fun〔fʌn〕*adj.* 好玩的；有趣的
guide〔gaɪd〕*n.* 導遊　　interest〔'ɪntrɪst〕*n.* 興趣

11. Let's start out early tomorrow.

Let's start out early tomorrow.	我們明天早點出發。
I'll pick you up at seven-thirty.	我會在七點半開車去接你。
I'll be there on time.	我會準時到那裡。
Please meet me out front.	請在門口和我見面。
I'll be waiting in the car.	我會在車子裡面等你。
I'll keep driving around if I can't park.	如果我沒辦法停車的話，我就會不停地繞圈子。
Don't eat anything before.	你先不要吃任何東西。
I'll take you for a good breakfast.	我將帶你去吃一頓豐盛的早餐。
Your batteries will be fully charged.	你將會充滿活力。

BOOK 10

**

start out 動身；出發　　***pick sb. up*** 開車接某人
on time 準時　　meet〔mɪt〕*v.* 和…見面
out front 在門外　　***keep + V-ing*** 一直…；不停地…
around〔ə'raʊnd〕*adv.* 兜著圈子
park〔pɑrk〕*v.* 停車　　battery〔'bætərɪ〕*n.* 電池
fully〔'fʊlɪ〕*adv.* 完全地　　charge〔tʃɑrdʒ〕*v.* 使充電

BOOK 10

12. *I'm sorry you're leaving.*

I'm sorry you're leaving.	我很遺憾你要離開了。
I enjoyed your visit.	和你在一起的這段時間很愉快。
I look forward to seeing you again.	我盼望能再見到你。
Come back anytime.	請隨時回來。
You're always welcome.	隨時歡迎你。
You have an open invitation.	隨時歡迎你。
Have a safe trip.	希望你旅途平安。
Have a nice flight.	祝你飛行順利。
Take care returning home.	回家路上要小心。

**─────────────

sorry〔'sɔrɪ〕*adj.* 遺憾的　　enjoy〔ɪn'dʒɔɪ〕*v.* 喜歡；享受
visit〔'vɪzɪt〕*n.* 拜訪；逗留；作客　　*look forward to* 盼望；期待
anytime〔'ɛnɪ,taɪm〕*adv.* 在任何時候；隨時
welcome〔'wɛlkəm〕*adj.* 受歡迎的
open〔'opən〕*adj.* 沒有時間限制的
invitation〔,ɪnvə'teʃən〕*n.* 邀請函
safe〔sef〕*adj.* 安全的　　flight〔flaɪt〕*n.* 飛行
take care 注意；小心　　return〔rɪ'tɜn〕*v.* 返回

唸英文要像唸經一樣，每天大聲唸，從起床到睡覺，唸得比看得快，最後不看也會唸，養成習慣後，你會全身舒爽，你試試看，奇妙無比。

1. When are you arriving?
   What's the date and time?
   What's your airline and flight
     number?

   What are your plans?
   Do you have reservations?
   Shall I book a room for you?

   It's fall here.
   The weather is getting colder.
   Please pack some warm clothes.

2. Welcome!
   You made it!
   I'm glad you're here.

   I'm pleased to meet you.
   I've heard so much about you.
   It's an honor.

   How was your flight?
   How are you feeling?
   What shall we do first?

3. Shall we go now?
   I have a car outside.
   Please follow me.

   Let me help.
   Let me carry that.
   I insist.

   Here's the car.
   Bags go in the trunk.
   Hop in.

4. First time here?
   Been here before?
   Have any questions?

   Are you tired at all?
   Are you hungry or thirsty?
   If you need anything, let me know.

   How do you like this weather?
   Is it different?
   Is it like this back home?

5. *I* beg your pardon?
   I didn't catch that.
   What did you say?

   Could you repeat that?
   Could you speak up?
   Please speak slowly.

   I don't get it.
   What do you mean?
   Please explain it to me.

6. Here's the schedule.
   Take a look.
   See if it's OK.

   I'd like your opinion.
   I want your approval.
   You can change it if you want.

   Let's discuss it.
   Let's go over it.
   I want everything to be clear.

7. How about a meal?
   Let me invite you.
   I know some good places.

   You'll like it.
   You'll have fun.
   It'll be a good time.

   Do you have time?
   We won't be gone long.
   You're welcome to join me.

8. Order anything.
   Choose what you like.
   Don't worry about the price.

   This dish is a house favorite.
   I've had it before.
   It's very tasty.

   How is it?
   Is it good?
   Want some more?

9. Are you all right?
   Is anything the matter?
   Is everything OK?

   You look a little pale.
   You must be exhausted.
   I bet you're tired.

   Can I get you anything?
   Want to take some medicine?
   Do you want me to take you to
      the doctor?

10. What are you doing this weekend?
    Have any plans?
    Want to meet?

    I have some free time.
    Want to go sightseeing?
    Want to do something fun?

    Let me be your guide.
    What are your interests?
    What do you want to do?

11. Let's start out early tomorrow.
    I'll pick you up at seven-thirty.
    I'll be there on time.

    Please meet me out front.
    I'll be waiting in the car.
    I'll keep driving around if I can't
       park.

    Don't eat anything before.
    I'll take you for a good breakfast.
    Your batteries will be fully charged

12. *I*'m sorry you're leaving.
    I enjoyed your visit.
    I look forward to seeing you again

    Come back anytime.
    You're always welcome.
    You have an open invitation.

    Have a safe trip.
    Have a nice flight.
    Take care returning home.

BOOK 11 當一個好客人

▶11-1 當你想去朋友家拜訪時，就可以打電話跟他說：

> Hey, it's me.
> How the heck are you?
> It's been a while.

▶11-2 當你一進朋友家的時候，就說：

> My, your home is gorgeous.
> It looks so inviting.
> It feels warm and friendly.

▶11-3 進到客廳後，坐在沙發上，就可說：

> I like the decoration.
> It's very stylish.
> It has a comfortable feel.

▶11-4 看到朋友的傢俱，就可說：

> Your furniture is lovely.
> Every piece is attractive.
> It really makes the room.

▶11-5 當你一走進廚房，就可說：

> Your kitchen is modern.
> You have more shelves and cabinets.
> It's much nicer than mine.

▶11-6 快要吃飯時，看到主人忙裡忙外，就可以說：

> Put me to work.
> Give me something to do.
> If you don't let me help, I'll feel guilty.

▶11-7 坐在餐桌吃飯時，你就可以說：

> This smells marvelous.
> The aroma is incredible.
> It looks too good to eat.

▶11-8 看到主人可愛的小baby，就可說：

> What a cute baby!
> What a little angel!
> What an adorable child!

▶11-9 看到主人的小孩，就可說：

> You have a great kid.
> He looks like you.
> He looks intelligent and bright.

▶11-10 看到主人家的狗，就可說：

> What a great-looking dog!
> What a perfect companion!
> Is it a he or she?

▶11-11 看到主人有這麼好的家庭，就可說：

> Look at you.
> You have it all.
> You've got everything.

▶11-12 要告別時，在門口，你就可說：

> You are a wonderful host.
> Thanks for your hospitality.
> Thanks for having me over.

1. *Hey, it's me.*

Hey, it's me.	嘿，是我。
How the heck are you?	你究竟怎樣？
It's been a while.	自從我們上次見面以來，已經很久了。
I'm coming to your area.	我要到你家附近。
I'll be in your neck of the woods.	我將去你那邊。
I'm anxious to see you.	我急於想見你。
Can I come over?	我能不能順便拜訪你？
Are you up for a visitor?	方便去拜訪你嗎？
We can catch up on things.	我們可以聊聊近況。

**

hey〔he〕*interj.* 嘿；喂；啊　　heck〔hɛk〕*n.* hell 的委婉語
the heck 究竟；到底　　while〔hwaɪl〕*n.* 一會兒；一段時間
area〔'ɛrɪə〕*n.* 地區；地方　　neck〔nɛk〕*n.* 脖子；狹長地帶
neck of the woods 地帶；地段；附近地區
anxious〔'æŋkʃəs〕*adj.* 渴望的　　*come over* 順便拜訪
catch up on 得到關於…的消息；趕完（應完成的工作）

2. Can I have a tour?

My, your home is gorgeous.	哎呀，你家好美啊。
It looks so inviting.	它看起來非常吸引人。
It feels warm and friendly.	它使人感覺既溫暖又親切。
It's very charming.	它非常迷人。
I'd love to see more.	我很想要多看一點。
Can I have a tour?	我能不能參觀一下？
It's a nice neighborhood.	它在好的地段。
It's peaceful and quiet.	這裡非常安靜。
How did you find this place?	你是怎麼找到這個地方的？

BOOK 11

**

my〔maɪ〕*interj.*【表示驚訝】哎喲；哎呀
gorgeous〔'gɔrdʒəs〕*adj.* 華麗的；極美的
inviting〔ɪn'vaɪtɪŋ〕*adj.* 吸引人的
feel〔fil〕*v.* 使人感覺　　warm〔wɔrm〕*adj.* 溫暖的
friendly〔'frɛndlɪ〕*adj.* 友善的；親切的
charming〔'tʃɑrmɪŋ〕*adj.* 迷人的；吸引人的
tour〔tʊr〕*n.* 參觀
neighborhood〔'nebəˌhʊd〕*n.* 鄰近地區；地段
peaceful〔'pisfəl〕*adj.* 平靜的　　quiet〔'kwaɪət〕*adj.* 安靜的

3. I like the decoration.

I like the decoration.	我喜歡這種裝潢。
It's very stylish.	它非常有格調。
It has a comfortable feel.	它給我舒適的感覺。
The lighting is just right.	燈光剛好。
All the colors flow well.	所有的顏色都很搭配。
It creates a relaxed atmosphere.	它創造了一個溫暖而輕鬆的氣氛。
You have a good eye.	你很有眼光。
You have good taste.	你有好的品味。
I should hire you to do my house.	我應該雇用你來裝潢我的房子。

BOOK 11

** ────────────

decoration〔ˌdɛkə'reʃən〕*n.* 裝飾；裝潢
stylish〔'staɪlɪʃ〕*adj.* 有格調的；有氣派的
feel〔fil〕*n.* 感覺　　lighting〔'laɪtɪŋ〕*n.* 照明；光線
just right 剛好　　flow〔flo〕*v.* 流動；流暢；順利進行
create〔krɪ'et〕*v.* 創造　　relaxed〔rɪ'lækst〕*adj.* 輕鬆的
atmosphere〔'ætməsˌfɪr〕*n.* 大氣；氣氛
eye〔aɪ〕*n.* 鑑別力；眼光　　taste〔test〕*n.* 品味；鑑賞力
hire〔haɪr〕*v.* 雇用　　do〔du〕*v.* 裝潢；佈置

4. *Your furniture is lovely.*

Your furniture is lovely.	你的傢俱很漂亮。
Every piece is attractive.	每一件都吸引人。
It really makes the room.	它真的造就了這個房間。
That's a fabulous table.	那張桌子很棒。
Those chairs look fantastic.	那些椅子看起來很棒。
What type of wood is that?	那是哪一種木頭？
This couch feels great.	這個沙發給人的感覺真棒。
I like the material.	我喜歡這個材料。
The fabric is so soft and	這個布料非常柔軟而且
smooth.	光滑。

** ———————————————

furniture〔ˋfɝnɪtʃɚ〕*n.* 傢俱
lovely〔ˋlʌvlɪ〕*adj.* 可愛的；漂亮的　　piece〔pis〕*n.* 一件
attractive〔əˋtræktɪv〕*adj.* 吸引人的
fabulous〔ˋfæbjələs〕*adj.* 很棒的；極好的
fantastic〔fænˋtæstɪk〕*adj.* 極好的；很棒的
type〔taɪp〕*n.* 類型；種類　　wood〔wʊd〕*n.* 木材；木頭
couch〔kaʊtʃ〕*n.* (長)沙發　　material〔məˋtɪrɪəl〕*n.* 材料
fabric〔ˋfæbrɪk〕*n.* 織物；織品；布料
soft〔sɔft〕*adj.* 柔軟的　　smooth〔smuð〕*adj.* 平滑的；光滑的

5. *Complimenting Different Rooms*

Your kitchen is modern.	你的廚房很現代化。
You have more shelves and cabinets.	你有比較多的架子和櫥櫃。
It's much nicer than mine.	它比我的好很多。
Your bedrooms are cozy.	你的臥室很溫馨。
Your closets are roomy.	你的衣櫥很大。
The carpet is thick and plush.	地毯又厚又豪華。
The living room is my favorite.	客廳是我最喜愛的。
It's the highlight of the house.	它是這個房子最好的部份。
Thank you for showing me around.	謝謝你帶我參觀。

BOOK 11

**

modern〔ˋmɑdən〕*adj.* 現代化的   shelf〔ʃɛlf〕*n.* 架子
cabinet〔ˋkæbənɪt〕*n.* 櫥櫃   nice〔naɪs〕*adj.* 好的
bedroom〔ˋbɛd͵rum〕*n.* 臥室   cozy〔ˋkozɪ〕*adj.* 溫暖而舒適的
closet〔ˋklɑzɪt〕*n.* 衣櫥;衣櫃   roomy〔ˋrumɪ〕*adj.* 寬敞的
carpet〔ˋkɑrpɪt〕*n.* 地毯   thick〔θɪk〕*adj.* 厚的
plush〔plʌʃ〕*adj.* 豪華的   favorite〔ˋfevərɪt〕*n.* 最喜歡的人或物
highlight〔ˋhaɪ͵laɪt〕*n.* 最重要的部份;最好的部份
show sb. *around* 帶某人參觀

6. *Put me to work*.

Put me to work.	讓我工作。
Give me something to do.	給我一點事情做。
If you don't let me help,	如果你不讓我幫忙,我會
I'll feel guilty.	覺得有罪惡感。
Let me set the table.	讓我來擺餐具。
Where are the plates?	盤子在哪裡?
Where do you keep your	你的餐具放在哪裡?
silverware?	
You made the meal.	你做了飯。
I'll clear the table.	我來收拾桌子。
I'll do the dishes.	我來洗碗盤。

BOOK 11

**

put〔pʊt〕v. 使做某事　　guilty〔'gɪltɪ〕adj. 有罪惡感的;內疚的
set the table 擺好餐具,準備開飯　　plate〔plet〕n. 盤子
silverware〔'sɪlvə‚wɛr〕n. 銀製餐具;銀白色金屬餐具
make〔mek〕v. 做(飯);烹煮　　meal〔mil〕n. 一餐
clear〔klɪr〕v. 清理;收拾　　*clear the table* 收拾桌子
do〔du〕v. 使清潔;洗滌　　dish〔dɪʃ〕n. 盤子
the dishes 餐桌用杯盤類　　*do the dishes* 洗碗盤

7. *This smells marvelous*.

This smells marvelous.	這個聞起來很香。
The aroma is incredible.	味道聞起來太香了。
It looks too good to eat.	它太好了，我捨不得吃。
Every bite is delightful.	每一口都好吃。
I've never had better.	我從來沒吃過更好的。
This really takes the cake.	這個真的是最好的。
My hat's off to you.	我對你表示敬意。
My compliments to the chef.	我向主廚致意。
What's the recipe?	怎麼做的？

** ————————————

smell〔smɛl〕*v.* 聞起來

marvelous〔'mɑrvḷəs〕*adj.* 令人驚嘆的；很棒的

aroma〔ə'romə〕*n.* 芳香；香氣

incredible〔ɪn'krɛdəbḷ〕*adj.* 令人難以置信的

bite〔baɪt〕*n.* （咬的）一口

delightful〔dɪ'laɪtfəl〕*adj.* 令人愉快的（= *enjoyable*）

have〔hæv〕*v.* 吃；喝 ***take the cake*** 得第一名；成爲最好的

compliment〔'kɑmpləmənt〕*n.* 稱讚；(*pl.*) 問候；致意

chef〔ʃɛf〕*n.* 主廚 recipe〔'rɛsəpɪ〕*n.* 烹飪法；食譜

BOOK 11

8. What a cute baby!

What a cute baby!	多麼可愛的小孩！
What a little angel!	多麼可愛的小天使！
What an adorable child!	多麼討人喜歡的孩子！
How old is your baby?	你的小孩多大了？
How many months?	幾個月大？
Is it a boy or a girl?	它是男孩還是女孩？
Hi there, sweetie.	嗨，小可愛。
How about a smile?	笑一個怎麼樣？
Can I hold him?	我可不可以抱他？

**

cute〔kjut〕*adj.* 可愛的　　　angel〔'endʒəl〕*n.* 天使
adorable〔ə'dorəbḷ〕*adj.* 可愛的
hi there【招呼語】嗨；你（們）好
sweetie〔'swɪtɪ〕*n.* 心愛的人；親愛的人
How about~? ～如何？　　smile〔smaɪl〕*n.* 微笑
hold〔hold〕*v.* 抓住；抱著

BOOK 11

9. *You have a great kid*.

You have a great kid.	你的小孩很棒。
He looks like you.	他看起來像你。
He looks intelligent and bright.	他看起來非常聰明。
He's very polite.	他很有禮貌。
He acts mature for his age.	以他的年齡來說,他的舉止很成熟。
You've raised him well.	你把他教得很好。
Kids are a handful.	小孩眞麻煩。
Your child turned out swell.	你的小孩變得很好。
You must be a good parent.	你一定是個好的父(母)親。

BOOK 11

** —————————————

kid〔kɪd〕*n.* 小孩　　intelligent〔ɪn'tɛlədʒənt〕*adj.* 聰明的
bright〔braɪt〕*adj.* 聰明的　　polite〔pə'laɪt〕*adj.* 有禮貌的
act〔ækt〕*v.* 舉止　　mature〔mə'tʃʊr, mə'tjʊr〕*adj.* 成熟的
raise〔rez〕*v.* 養育;敎養
handful〔'hænd,fʊl〕*n.* 難控制的人或物;麻煩的事
turn out 結果變成　　swell〔swɛl〕*adj.* 極好的;出色的
must〔mʌst〕*aux.* 一定　　parent〔'pɛrənt, 'pærənt〕*n.* 父;母

10. *What a great-looking dog!*

What a great-looking dog!	多麼漂亮的狗！
What a perfect companion!	多麼好的同伴！
Is it a he or she?	牠是公的還是母的？
What's his name?	牠的名字是什麼？
What breed is he?	牠是什麼品種？
Can he do any tricks?	牠會不會表演任何把戲？
Come here, fella.	過來吧，狗狗。
Don't be afraid.	不要害怕。
I won't hurt you.	我不會傷害你。

**

---

great-looking〔'gret'lʊkɪŋ〕 *adj.* 漂亮的
perfect〔'pɝfɪkt〕 *adj.* 完美的
companion〔kəm'pænjən〕 *n.* 同伴；夥伴
he〔hi〕 *n.* 男性；雄性動物   she〔ʃi〕 *n.* 女性；雌性動物
breed〔brid〕 *n.* 品種   trick〔trɪk〕 *n.* 把戲
do tricks 表演把戲   fella〔'fɛlə〕 *n.* 夥伴；小伙子
afraid〔ə'fred〕 *adj.* 害怕的   hurt〔hɝt〕 *v.* 傷害

BOOK 11

11. I admire you.

Look at you.	你看看。
You have it all.	你什麼都有。
You've got everything.	你什麼都有了。
You have a terrific home.	你的家很棒。
You have an excellent job.	你有很好的工作。
You're really moving up.	你真的步步高升。
I admire you.	我欽佩你。
I envy you.	我羨慕你。
I wish I were you.	我希望我是你。

** ————————————

look at 看   *have it all* 什麼都有
you've got 你有 (= *you have*)
terrific〔təˋrɪfɪk〕*adj.* 很棒的
excellent〔ˋɛksḷənt〕*adj.* 極好的   *move up* 晉升；前進
admire〔ədˋmaɪr〕*v.* 欽佩；讚賞；羨慕
envy〔ˋɛnvɪ〕*v.* 羨慕；嫉妒   wish〔wɪʃ〕*v.* 希望

12. *You are a wonderful host.*

You are a wonderful host.	你很好客。
Thanks for your hospitality.	謝謝你的款待。
Thanks for having me over.	謝謝你邀請我來。
Now you owe me a visit.	現在你要記得,要來我家玩。
Next time, it's my turn.	下一次輪到我了。
I want to repay your kindness.	我想要報答你親切的招待。
It's been real.	眞是愉快。
I had a ball.	我玩得很愉快。
I'll be seeing you.	我會再見到你。

** ———————————————

wonderful〔'wʌndɚfəl〕*adj.* 很棒的　　host〔host〕*n.* 主人
hospitality〔ˌhɑspɪ'tælətɪ〕*n.* 款待;熱情招待;好客
have sb. over 請某人到家裡來作客
owe〔o〕*v.* 欠　　visit〔'vɪzɪt〕*n.* 拜訪;作客
turn〔tɝn〕*n.* 輪値;輪班　　repay〔rɪ'pe〕*v.* 報答
kindness〔'kaɪndnɪs〕*n.* 親切;親切的行爲;親切的態度
real〔'riəl〕*adj.* 眞正的　　ball〔bɔl〕*n.* 愉快的時刻

唸英文要像唸經一樣，每天大聲唸，從起床到睡覺，唸得比看得快，最後不看也會唸，養成習慣後，你會全身舒爽，你試試看，奇妙無比。

1. Hey, it's me.
   How the heck are you?
   It's been a while.

   I'm coming to your area.
   I'll be in your neck of the woods.
   I'm anxious to see you.

   Can I come over?
   Are you up for a visitor?
   We can catch up on things.

2. My, your home is gorgeous.
   It looks so inviting.
   It feels warm and friendly.

   It's very charming.
   I'd love to see more.
   Can I have a tour?

   It's a nice neighborhood.
   It's peaceful and quiet.
   How did you find this place?

3. I like the decoration.
   It's very stylish.
   It has a comfortable feel.

   The lighting is just right.
   All the colors flow well.
   It creates a relaxed atmosphere.

   You have a good eye.
   You have good taste.
   I should hire you to do my house.

4. Your furniture is lovely.
   Every piece is attractive.
   It really makes the room.

   That's a fabulous table.
   Those chairs look fantastic.
   What type of wood is that?

   This couch feels great.
   I like the material.
   The fabric is so soft and smooth.

5. Your kitchen is modern.
   You have more shelves and cabinets.
   It's much nicer than mine.

   Your bedrooms are cozy.
   Your closets are roomy.
   The carpet is thick and plush.

   The living room is my favorite.
   It's the highlight of the house.
   Thank you for showing me around.

6. Put me to work.
   Give me something to do.
   If you don't let me help, I'll feel guilty.

   Let me set the table.
   Where are the plates?
   Where do you keep your silverware?

   You made the meal.
   I'll clear the table.
   I'll do the dishes.

7. This smells marvelous.
   The aroma is incredible.
   It looks too good to eat.

   Every bite is delightful.
   I've never had better.
   This really takes the cake.

   My hat's off to you.
   My compliments to the chef.
   What's the recipe?

8. *What* a cute baby!
   What a little angel!
   What an adorable child!

   How old is your baby?
   How many months?
   Is it a boy or a girl?

   Hi there, sweetie.
   How about a smile?
   Can I hold him?

9. You have a great kid.
   He looks like you.
   He looks intelligent and bright.

   He's very polite.
   He acts mature for his age.
   You've raised him well.

   Kids are a handful.
   Your child turned out swell.
   You must be a good parent.

10. *What a* great-looking dog!
    What a perfect companion!
    Is it a he or she?

    What's his name?
    What breed is he?
    Can he do any tricks?

    Come here, fella.
    Don't be afraid.
    I won't hurt you.

11. Look at you.
    You have it all.
    You've got everything.

    You have a terrific home.
    You have an excellent job.
    You're really moving up.

    I admire you.
    I envy you.
    I wish I were you.

12. You are a wonderful host.
    Thanks for your hospitality.
    Thanks for having me over.

    Now you owe me a visit.
    Next time, it's my turn.
    I want to repay your kindness.

    It's been real.
    I had a ball.
    I'll be seeing you.

BOOK 12　當一個好主人

▶12-1　打電話給你的朋友，邀請他來你家作客，你可說：

> Come visit me.
> Pay me a visit.
> Call on me anytime.

▶12-2　朋友一進你家門，你就可說：

> Come on in.
> Step right inside.
> Here is a pair of slippers.

▶12-3　當朋友一坐下來，你就可說：

> My home is your home.
> Help yourself to anything.
> There's lots of stuff in the fridge.

▶12-4　可和朋友談論天氣，避免尷尬：

> What a scorcher!
> It's boiling outside.
> It's hotter than hell.

▶12-5　可和訪客談論近況，說：

> So, tell me your news.
> How have you been?
> Have you been keeping busy?

▶12-6　當看見你的朋友，因為你說的話而不高興的時候，就可說：

> Don't get me wrong.
> Don't get the wrong idea.
> I don't want you to misunderstand.

▶12-7 當你介紹你的太太給客人時，就可以說：

I'd like you to meet my wife.
She's my better half.
She's the brains of the family.

▶12-8 當你邀請客人留下來吃飯時，就可說：

Please stay for dinner.
Do me the honor.
Let's break bread together.

▶12-9 當大家一起吃飯時，你想敬酒，就可說：

Let me make a toast.
Let's have a drink together.
Here's to a fantastic future.

▶12-10 當你要請大家一起照相時，你就可說：

Let's take a snapshot.
Let's get a photo together.
It'll be a nice memory.

▶12-11 當你的客人要走的時候，你就可說：

Don't leave yet.
Don't go so soon.
Stay and talk some more.

▶12-12 餐會完了，送客的時候，你可說：

Thanks for coming.
Thanks for being my guest.
It was nice seeing you.

1. Come visit me.

Come visit me.	來我這裡玩。
Pay me a visit.	來我這裡玩。
Call on me anytime.	隨時來我這裡玩。
Drop in whenever.	隨時來我這裡玩。
Drop by when you can.	你有空就來玩。
Feel free to stop by.	不要客氣，來坐坐。
I'm inviting you now.	我現在邀請你。
My door is always open.	我永遠歡迎你。
Don't keep me waiting 　too long.	不要讓我等太久。

BOOK 12

**

visit〔'vɪzɪt〕*v.* 拜訪；遊覽；到（某人家）作客
pay sb. a visit 拜訪某人（= *visit*）　　*call on* 拜訪
anytime〔'ɛnɪ,taɪm〕*adv.* 隨時　　*drop in* 順道拜訪
whenever〔hwɛn'ɛvɚ〕*adv.* 無論何時
drop by 順道拜訪　　*feel free to V.* 請自由地…
stop by 順道拜訪　　invite〔ɪn'vaɪt〕*v.* 邀請

2. *Come on in*.

Come on in.	趕快進來。
Step right inside.	趕快進來。
Here is a pair of slippers.	這裡有一雙拖鞋。
Have a seat.	坐下來。
Sit down and relax.	坐下來休息休息。
Make yourself at home.	不要客氣。
You got here OK.	你順利到達這裡了。
How was the traffic?	交通狀況如何？
Any trouble finding this place?	找這個地方有沒有任何困難？

** ————————————

step〔stɛp〕*v.* 行走；踩；踏   right〔raɪt〕*adv.* 立刻；趕快
inside〔'ɪn'saɪd〕*adv.* 往裡面   *a pair of* 一雙
slippers〔'slɪpɚz〕*n. pl.* 拖鞋   *have a seat* 坐下
relax〔rɪ'læks〕*v.* 放鬆；休息
make oneself at home （像在家裡一樣）不拘束；覺得自在
OK〔'o'ke〕*adv.* 沒問題地；順利地
traffic〔'træfɪk〕*n.* 交通（量）
trouble〔'trʌbḷ〕*n.* 麻煩；困難

3. *My home is your home*.

My home is your home.	我的家就是你家。
Help yourself to anything.	自己拿任何東西。
There's lots of stuff in the fridge.	在冰箱裡有很多東西。
It's a little messy.	我家有點亂。
Please don't mind the clutter.	請不要介意凌亂。
We're pretty informal around here.	我們這裡非常隨便。
Wanna use the bathroom?	想不想要用廁所？
It's just down the hall.	它就在走道那一邊。
The switch is next to the door.	開關在門的旁邊。

**

help** oneself to* 自己取用   ***lots of 很多
stuff〔stʌf〕*n.* 東西   fridge〔frɪdʒ〕*n.* 冰箱
messy〔'mɛsɪ〕*adj.* 凌亂的   mind〔maɪnd〕*v.* 介意
clutter〔'klʌtɚ〕*n.* 凌亂；雜亂   pretty〔'prɪtɪ〕*adv.* 相當；非常
informal〔ɪn'fɔrml̩〕*adj.* 不正式的；隨便的
wanna〔'wɑnə〕*v.* 想要   bathroom〔'bæθ,rum〕*n.* 廁所
down〔daʊn〕*prep.* 在…那一邊   hall〔hɔl〕*n.* 走廊；走道
switch〔swɪtʃ〕*n.* 開關   ***next to*** 在…旁邊

4. *What a scorcher!*

What a scorcher!	好熱的天氣！
It's boiling outside.	外面天氣很熱。
It's hotter than hell.	眞是熱死人了。
This weather is so humid.	這個天氣非常潮濕。
It's so sticky.	天氣非常悶熱。
It makes me sweat like crazy.	它使我流很多汗。
I don't mind dry heat.	我不在乎乾熱的天氣。
It's the humidity I can't stand.	我沒辦法忍受潮濕的天氣。
The air is so damp and wet.	空氣非常潮濕。

BOOK 12

**

scorcher〔ˈskɔrtʃɚ〕*n.* 大熱天
boiling〔ˈbɔɪlɪŋ〕*adj.* 沸騰的；極熱的
hell〔hɛl〕*n.* 地獄　humid〔ˈhjumɪd〕*adj.* 潮濕的
sticky〔ˈstɪkɪ〕*adj.* 黏的；悶熱的　sweat〔swɛt〕*v.* 流汗
like crazy 瘋狂地；拼命地　mind〔maɪnd〕*v.* 介意；在乎
heat〔hit〕*n.* 熱　humidity〔hjuˈmɪdətɪ〕*n.* 潮濕
stand〔stænd〕*v.* 忍受　damp〔dæmp〕*adj.* 潮濕的

5. *So, tell me your news*.

So, tell me your news.	哦，告訴我你的近況。
How have you been?	你好嗎？
Have you been keeping busy?	你是不是一直很忙？
Are you working hard these days?	你最近有沒有努力啊？
Are you staying out of trouble?	你是不是平安？
Do you like what you're doing?	你是不是喜歡做你正在做的事？
I want to hear everything.	我想要聽到所有的事。
Don't skip a thing.	不要跳過任何一件事。
Don't leave anything out.	不要遺漏任何事。

**　BOOK 12**

** ─────────────

so〔so〕*adv.* 哦　　news〔njuz〕*n.* 新消息；新情況
keep〔kip〕*v.* 保持；持續　　*work hard* 努力
these days 最近　　*stay out of* 遠離
trouble〔ˈtrʌbḷ〕*n.* 麻煩　　skip〔skɪp〕*v.* 跳過；略過
leave out 遺漏；省略

6. *Don't get me wrong*.

Don't get me wrong.	不要誤會我。
Don't get the wrong idea.	不要會錯意。
I don't want you to misunderstand.	我不想要你誤解我。
Don't get mad.	不要生氣。
Don't take it seriously.	不要太認眞。
I didn't mean anything by it.	我這麼說沒什麼意思。
I was just kidding.	我只是在開玩笑。
I was just joking around.	我只是在開玩笑。
You know that's my style.	你知道那是我的作風。

BOOK 12

** ———————————————

get *sb.* ***wrong*** 誤解某人
misunderstand〔͵mɪsʌndə'stænd〕*v.* 誤解；誤會
mad〔mæd〕*adj.* 生氣的
seriously〔'sɪrɪəslɪ〕*adv.* 認眞地；嚴肅地
take~seriously 把～看得很認眞
mean〔min〕*v.* 意思是　　kid〔kɪd〕*v.* 開玩笑
joke〔dʒok〕*v.* 開玩笑　***joke around*** 開玩笑
style〔staɪl〕*n.* 風格；作風

7. *I'd like you to meet my wife.*

I'd like you to meet my wife.	我想要你認識我的太太。
She's my better half.	她是我的賢內助。
She's the brains of the family.	她是家裡的老大。
She runs the house.	她管理這個家。
She's an exceptional cook.	她很會煮飯。
I'd be lost without her.	如果沒有她，我不知道該怎麼辦。
She's a jack-of-all-trades.	她什麼都會。
She's an angel in disguise.	她像一個天使。
I couldn't ask for more.	我不能要求更多了。

BOOK 12

** ———————————————

meet〔mit〕*v.* 認識；和…見面
better half 賢內助；妻子；丈夫
brains〔brenz〕*n.* 聰明的人；領導者；中心人物
run〔rʌn〕*v.* 管理   exceptional〔ɪkˈsɛpʃənḷ〕*adj.* 傑出的
cook〔kʊk〕*n.* 廚師   lost〔lɔst〕*adj.* 不知所措的
jack-of-all-trades〔ˌdʒækəvˈɔlˌtredz〕*n.* 萬能先生；萬事通
angel〔ˈendʒəl〕*n.* 天使
disguise〔dɪsˈgaɪz〕*n.* 偽裝   ***ask for*** 要求

8. *Please stay for dinner*.

Please stay for dinner.	請留下來吃晚餐。
Do me the honor.	給我面子。
Let's break bread together.	我們一起吃飯吧。
You have no choice.	你沒有選擇的餘地。
I won't let you go.	我不會讓你走。
I won't take no for an answer.	我一定要你答應。
Don't make me beg.	不要讓我求你。
Do it for me.	幫我一個忙吧。
It would mean a lot to me.	這件事會對我很重要。

** ─────────

stay〔ste〕*v.* 停留　　do〔du〕*v.* 給予

honor〔'ɑnɚ〕*n.* 榮譽；榮幸　　bread〔brɛd〕*n.* 麵包

break bread 一起吃飯　　choice〔tʃɔɪs〕*n.* 選擇

take〔tek〕*v.* 接受　　beg〔bɛg〕*v.* 請求；懇求

mean〔min〕*v.* 意思是；有某種重要性

mean a lot 非常重要

9. Let me make a toast.

Let me make a toast.	讓我來敬酒吧。
Let's have a drink together.	我們一起喝一杯吧。
Here's to a fantastic future!	爲了美好的未來乾杯！
May you always be happy!	祝你永遠快樂！
May you always be lucky!	祝你永遠幸運！
May you live to be a hundred!	祝你活到一百歲！
Cheers!	乾杯！
Bottoms up!	乾杯！
Down the hatch!	乾杯！

** ─────────────

toast〔tost〕*n.* 乾杯；敬酒
have a drink 喝一杯（尤指酒）
Here's to…! 【敬酒時説】爲…乾杯！；祝…快樂、健康！
fantastic〔fæn'tæstɪk〕*adj.* 極好的
future〔'fjutʃɚ〕*n.* 未來　　may〔me〕*aux.* 但願…；祝…
happy〔'hæpɪ〕*adj.* 快樂的；幸福的
lucky〔'lʌkɪ〕*adj.* 幸運的　　cheers〔tʃɪrz〕*interj.* 乾杯
bottom〔'batəm〕*n.* 底　　*Bottoms up!* 乾杯！
hatch〔hætʃ〕*n.*（船的）艙口（蓋）
Down the hatch! 乾杯！

BOOK 12

10. *Let's take a snapshot*.

Let's take a snapshot.	我們照張相吧。
Let's get a photo together.	我們一起照張相吧。
It'll be a nice memory.	它將會是美好的回憶。
Could you please take our picture?	能不能請你替我們照張相？
My camera is easy to operate.	我的相機容易操作。
Just press this button.	只要按這個按鈕。
Hold still.	不要動。
Strike a pose.	擺出一個姿勢。
Smile and say cheese.	微笑，並且說 cheese。

**

snapshot〔'snæp,ʃɑt〕*n.* 快照；照片
photo〔'foto〕*n.* 相片   memory〔'mɛmərɪ〕*n.* 記憶；回憶
take one's picture 替某人照相
camera〔'kæmərə〕*n.* 照相機   operate〔'ɑpə,ret〕*v.* 操作
press〔prɛs〕*v.* 按；壓   button〔'bʌtn̩〕*n.* 按鈕
hold〔hold〕*v.* 維持   still〔stɪl〕*adj.* 靜止的；不動的
strike〔straɪk〕*v.* 擺出   pose〔poz〕*n.* 姿勢
cheese〔tʃiz〕*n.* 起司   *say cheese* 說 cheese；笑一個

BOOK 12

11. *Don't leave yet.*

Don't leave yet.	現在不要離開。
Don't go so soon.	不要這麼早走。
Stay and talk some more.	留下來再多聊一些。
What's *the* rush?	急什麼？
Why *the* hurry?	為什麼要這麼匆忙？
Where's *the* fire?	急什麼？
It's *still* early.	時間還早。
The night is *still* young.	天色還不是很晚。
You've got lots of time.	你有很多時間。

** ───────────

yet〔jɛt〕*adv.* 現在　　soon〔sun〕*adv.* 早；快

stay〔ste〕*v.* 停留　　rush〔rʌʃ〕*n.* 匆忙

hurry〔'hɝɪ〕*n.* 匆忙　　fire〔faɪr〕*n.* 火災

young〔jʌŋ〕*adj.* 尚早的

you've got 你有（= *you have*）　　*lots of* 很多

12. *Thanks for coming*.

Thanks for coming.	謝謝光臨。
Thanks for being my guest.	謝謝你來作客。
It was nice seeing you.	看到你眞好。
It's been delightful.	我們在一起一直很愉快。
I enjoyed every minute.	我每一分鐘都快樂。
I hate to see you go.	我眞不願意看你走。
Let's meet more often.	我們要更常見面吧。
Don't be a stranger.	不要不連絡。
Stay healthy, happy, and safe.	希望你保持健康、快樂，和平安。

**

guest〔gɛst〕*n.* 客人
delightful〔dɪˈlaɪtfəl〕*adj.* 愉快的；令人高興的
enjoy〔ɪnˈdʒɔɪ〕*v.* 喜歡；享受
hate〔het〕*v.* 眞不願意
stranger〔ˈstrendʒɚ〕*n.* 陌生人　　stay〔ste〕*v.* 保持
healthy〔ˈhɛlθɪ〕*adj.* 健康的　　safe〔sef〕*adj.* 安全的

BOOK 12

「一口氣背會話」經 BOOK 12

唸英文要像唸經一樣，每天大聲唸，從起床到睡覺，唸得比看得快，最後不看也會唸，養成習慣後，你會全身舒爽，你試試看，奇妙無比。

1. Come visit me.
   Pay me a visit.
   Call on me anytime.

   Drop in whenever.
   Drop by when you can.
   Feel free to stop by.

   I'm inviting you now.
   My door is always open.
   Don't keep me waiting too long.

2. Come on in.
   Step right inside.
   Here is a pair of slippers.

   Have a seat.
   Sit down and relax.
   Make yourself at home.

   You got here OK.
   How was the traffic?
   Any trouble finding this place?

3. My home is your home.
   Help yourself to anything.
   There's lots of stuff in the fridge.

   It's a little messy.
   Please don't mind the clutter.
   We're pretty informal around here.

   Wanna use the bathroom?
   It's just down the hall.
   The switch is next to the door.

4. What a scorcher!
   It's boiling outside.
   It's hotter than hell.

   This weather is so humid.
   It's so sticky.
   It makes me sweat like crazy.

   I don't mind dry heat.
   It's the humidity I can't stand.
   The air is so damp and wet.

5. So, tell me your news.
   How have you been?
   Have you been keeping busy?

   Are you working hard these days?
   Are you staying out of trouble?
   Do you like what you're doing?

   I want to hear everything.
   Don't skip a thing.
   Don't leave anything out.

6. *Don't get* me wrong.
   Don't get the wrong idea.
   I don't want you to misunderstand.

   Don't get mad.
   Don't take it seriously.
   I didn't mean anything by it.

   I was just kidding.
   I was just joking around.
   You know that's my style.

7. I'd like you to meet my wife.
   She's my better half.
   She's the brains of the family.

   She runs the house.
   She's an exceptional cook.
   I'd be lost without her.

   She's a jack-of-all-trades.
   She's an angel in disguise.
   I couldn't ask for more.

8. Please stay for dinner.
   Do me the honor.
   Let's break bread together.

   You have no choice.
   I won't let you go.
   I won't take no for an answer.

   Don't make me beg.
   Do it for me.
   It would mean a lot to me.

9. *Let* me make a toast.
   Let's have a drink together.
   Here's to a fantastic future!

   May you always be happy!
   May you always be lucky!
   May you live to be a hundred!

   Cheers!
   Bottoms up!
   Down the hatch!

10. *Let's* take a snapshot.
    Let's get a photo together.
    It'll be a nice memory.

    Could you please take our picture
    My camera is easy to operate.
    Just press this button.

    Hold still.
    Strike a pose.
    Smile and say cheese.

11. *Don't* leave yet.
    Don't go so soon.
    Stay and talk some more.

    What's *the* rush?
    Why *the* hurry?
    Where's *the* fire?

    It's *still* early.
    The night is *still* young.
    You've got lots of time.

12. *Thanks for* coming.
    Thanks for being my guest.
    It was nice seeing you.

    It's been delightful.
    I enjoyed every minute.
    I hate to see you go.

    Let's meet more often.
    Don't be a stranger.
    Stay healthy, happy, and safe.

　　　剛開始背「一口氣背會話」，也許困難一點。只要堅持下去，一旦學會背快的技巧，就能一本接一本地背下去。每一本108句背到1分鐘之內，就變成直覺，終生不會忘記，唯有不忘記，才能不斷地累積。

「一口氣背會話」1,296 句索引

索
引

索
引

索
引

索
引

索
引

索
引

索
引

每一句都是精挑細選的
美國口語精華，
背完立刻會說。

你想說英文嗎？
用背的語言
說起來最有信心。

一開始背，

你就不會無聊，

就沒有煩惱，

每天都有成就感。

學英文最簡單的方法，
就是背短句。
背得越多，
你越會說。